CALL ME AMY

MARCIA STRYKOWSKI

LUMINIS BOOKS

LUMINIS BOOKS
Published by Luminis Books
1950 East Greyhound Pass, #18, PMB 280,
Carmel, Indiana, 46033, U.S.A.

PUBLISHER'S NOTICE
This is a work of fiction. Names, characters, places, and incidents are either the product of the author's imagination or are used fictitiously. Any resemblance to actual persons, living or dead, business establishments, events, or locales is entirely coincidental.

Cover Photo & Author Photo by Thompson Photography & Graphic Design. Cover design by Joanne Riske.

Hardcover ISBN: 978-1-935462-76-7
Paperback ISBN: 978-1-935462-75-0

Printed in the United States of America

10 9 8 7 6 5 4 3 2 1

For my parents,
Raymond and Margaret Sorensen,
with love and gratitude.

Early praise for *Call Me Amy:*

"A wounded seal pup propels 13-year-old Amy Henderson into an unlikely alliance with an unusual older woman and a mysterious boy in a small Maine fishing village. Readers will cheer for Amy as she protects Pup, gains confidence, faces challenges, and comes up with an idea that could change not only the future of her village, but also her own life. With a skillful hand, Strykowski introduces us to a small town with memorable characters and the girl who could bring them all together."

—Anne Broyles, award-winning author of *Priscilla and the Hollyhocks*

"In a small town in Maine in the 1970's, Amy is standing on the brink of becoming a young adult. The events that will force her to discover who she is, what she is made of and how she wants others to perceive her are sweetly told through awkward teenage moments, the triumphs and sadnesses of that age and, ultimately, Amy's discovery of her own beliefs, strength and courage."

—Kathleen Benner Duble, acclaimed author of *The Sacrifice*

Early praise for *Call Me Amy:*

"Well-drawn, sympathetic characters and the developing spark between Amy and Craig combine to create a pleasant, satisfying read."

—*Kirkus*

"Strykowski ably depicts Amy's insecurity and self-doubt, Craig's bravura and pain, and Miss Cogshell's wisdom with a deft, convincing touch. In essence, Amy comes of age as she fights to find her voice in the outside world and shed some of her debilitating insecurity. Readers will cheer her on, and her splendid team too."

—*Booklist*

Acknowledgments

Along with Mom and Dad, thank you to Bette, Bob, Derek, and Marla for your ongoing love and support. And special thanks to all the writers and readers who read *Call Me Amy* in its various stages. Also, thank you to Tracy Richardson and Chris Katsaropoulos of Luminis Books.

CALL ME AMY

1

SHARP OCEAN AIR raced around my bedroom before I slammed the windows shut and headed downstairs.

My big sister Nancy called out to me. "Are you going for a walk by yourself again?" She swung her dark, glossy ponytail over one straight shoulder.

I nodded as I stooped to pull on my boots.

Nancy, as different from me as perfume is to tiddlywinks, was sprawled across the kitchen linoleum. *Seventeen* magazine lay open while Carly Simon's hit song "You're So Vain" blared from her transistor radio. Nancy had little wads of cotton stuffed between her toes, so her shiny, pink toenails wouldn't smudge. I blocked my nose, hoping to get out of there fast before the smell of nail polish made me puke.

"You know, Amy, you really should try to make some friends—so you don't have to mope around by yourself every Saturday. There must be *somebody* else your age in this boring port."

Duh. What was I supposed to say to that?

"I'm telling you," continued Nancy, raising her voice over the music as she examined her toes, "just two more years and I'll kiss this hole-in-the-wall town goodbye."

I slipped into my yellow parka and pushed open the door, ignoring her. The breeze swept in to flip the pages of Nancy's magazine.

"Check the post office for me!" Nancy's shout came faint against the wind just before the door blew shut.

I was already halfway down the hill, and most likely I would end up at the post office. Where else would I go? In Port Wells there were only so many places to visit, so the pier, Al's General Store, and the post office were at the top of the list. For the religious sort, there was a Baptist church across from the post office. Its steeple was the first thing you'd spot when coming around the corner off the main road.

Oh, and how could I forget—for those who liked smelly little bait shops, there was one of those, sticking off the back of the general store. A simple thing like wanting to buy a pair of bellbottoms or borrow a library book meant going into Thomaston—thirty miles away. The sparkle of the salt air and surf made living on the coast all worth it, though.

I slowed my pace and took tiny steps down the hill through the pine trees, my boots flattening the last of the snow. As much as I hated to admit it, I knew Nancy was right. So far, 1973 had been a lonely year.

My best, or I guess you could say only friend moved away last spring and had turned out to be a lousy letter writer. Like, none at all. I had spent half the summer hanging around the post office waiting for a letter, postcard, *anything*, until I finally gave up sending my own weekly letters.

Now, after being stuck inside most of the winter, people were poking their heads out. Port Wells was slowly coming alive again. A couple of townies were home safe from Vietnam and folks seemed more relaxed. There was a hint of spring in the air. Just a hint—for in Maine, spring was sluggish. Colors were as vivid as a new tin of watercolor paints: viridian green trees against cobalt blue with zinc white clouds. I could hear the Percy boys shrieking out baseball calls from the village field.

I looked back up the hill, through the pines, at our Victorian-style house and inhaled the damp, salt air. Years ago my great-grandparents had come to Port Wells to build up their health. They used to say if they could only bottle this fresh atmosphere and sell it as medicine, then they'd be millionaires. They swore by it, and us Hendersons had been here ever since.

Down at the base of our hill I found an open area that was almost green and bare of snow. I flipped a cartwheel. The coarse ground left tiny pebble dents in my palms. I rubbed them together and flipped again, the rush of freedom outweighing any pain.

Then I heard a few dull claps. I spun around, peeked through my tangled hair, and found Craig Miller sitting halfway up a tree applauding me. Great. I couldn't see all of him, mostly just his old army jacket. He wore it every single day.

"Encore, Shrimp, encore." Ugh, I hated that nickname. Craig scrunched down to peer through the branches at me. My face felt hot. I glanced at an imaginary watch on my wrist, as though late for some important event. The last thing I wanted to see was his foolish grin.

Craig was one of those tough kids whom all the boy-crazy girls giggled about, although he never seemed to notice. Too cool, I guess. He'd been in my class since first grade and even though we were in eighth grade now, I still didn't feel comfortable with him. I usually ended up in the desk beside him because teachers thought it clever to put a silent student, like me, next to a big mouth like him. It's not like I chose to be silent; I just never had anything to say that someone wasn't already saying.

Craig had no problem spitting out whatever came into his head and it was sometimes hard to tell if he was joking or not. He was only one of the kids who called me Shrimp on a regular basis. I'm not sure when or why it started. I mean, I knew I was small for my age, but did that give everybody the right to compare me to a slimy piece of seafood?

I heard a low chuckle from the tree and took off, glancing over one shoulder to make sure I wasn't being followed—fat chance—as I raced across the field between baseball innings. The players, all three of them, were taking a break. When I reached the pier I slowed down to catch my breath.

I could make out Wàwàckèchi Island sharp in the distance, and could almost see the lighthouse, a vague shape jutting upwards. Most mornings the fog came in so thick, you wouldn't even know an island was out there. There was never a time I could pass by the ocean without stopping to stare, and, for all its blemishes, I truly believed Port Wells to be the most beautiful place on earth.

Today the water was calm with a few dinghies drifting on the horizon. The mail boat, surrounded by chunks of ice, waited by the pier. Soon it would make its daily trip out to Wàwàckèchi. On the other side of the wharf, an old fisherman in slippery yellow coveralls was squatting down by a bucket of red paint that would bring stripes to a long row of lobster buoys. I watched a minute, and then moved on.

Even Old Coot's house didn't look quite so drab on a day like this. But I still stayed way over on the opposite side of the lane—just in case.

Before I got to the post office, I stopped to watch three girls a little bit younger than me who were hanging around the gas pump outside Al's General Store.

Out of the corner of my eye I could see them gesturing and pulling at each other, talking and laughing like there was no tomorrow. I wondered what in the world they could be talking about. What did anyone talk about besides homework assignments or the weather? They were probably too young to be discussing Nixon's Watergate problems. Would these girls clam up like I did, around the time they got their first zit? Probably not. Might as well face it, I was doomed to be an outcast forever. I found a smooth white pebble and kicked it along until it bounced off the wooden steps of the post office.

As I pushed open the post office door, smells of musty paper lunged from the darkened corners. Sally Johnson, the most chipper postmistress in the world, greeted me.

"Well, hello there, Miss Nancy. How is everything up on your hill?"

"I'm Amy."

"What's that?"

"Amy," I whispered. Since I'd been going to school with her snotty daughter, Pamela, for all of my life, you'd think she'd at least know my name by now. I shifted my weight and fiddled with my parka's zipper pull.

"Well, yes, let's see. I think we have some mail here for your family." She paused, stuck one finger in her ear, and glanced around at the small stacks of mail.

"Ah, here it is," she announced as she examined her finger for wax. I looked away disgusted, and wondered why there couldn't be a more pleasant place to visit. Everyone knew that Sally listened in on telephone party lines and for all we knew she probably read the mail too, sealing it up again with her earwax. Yuck. I shivered, then realized she was talking to me.

" . . . hasn't picked up her mail lately and it's piling up. You'll be going right by Miss Cogshell's place." Sally peered at the envelopes as if deciding whether she approved of their contents. "I'll put all this in a rubber band and you can bring it over there."

My mouth fell open. Miss Cogshell was Old Coot! The most terrifying person in Port Wells and I was supposed to casually drop in on her? "But . . . "

Sally had already turned her back and didn't hear my timid protest. With clammy hands I took the extra bundle and headed out the door.

2

GOING TO OLD Coot's house had even less appeal than painting my toenails. I could recall bits and pieces of gossip about the old lady who lived at the end of the road. She was the largest, scariest, most ugly woman we kids had ever seen. From the safety of the school bus windows, the kids all said she was a witch and called her Old Coot. I never called her anything, out loud. I always sat at the front of the bus, second seat on the right, staring straight ahead for the whole long ride—halfway to Thomaston. Old Coot didn't venture out much, except for short walks back and forth to the general store. She used an odd-looking cane on those excursions.

I decided my best bet would be to leave her mail by the door and run. I glanced at my own pile. One was addressed to Nancy in scribbled handwriting. I rolled my eyes. Must be that gross boy she met last summer at camp. I held the envelope up towards where the sun had been, hoping to read it, but no luck. "Amy," I could picture Nancy's voice saying, "you're getting as nosy as Postmistress Sally."

There were several bills and letters for my parents. Without meaning to, I began peeking through Miss Cogshell's large bundle of mail. Exotic stamps were on several of them—France, England, Africa. Who would write to her?

Soon I found myself in front of the small house by the pier. The sun had slipped behind the clouds, and turned the sea a dull grey. Miss Cogshell's place, weathered from ocean winds, always appeared dark and dreary. A tiny, enclosed widow's walk stuck out from the top of her roof. Its only window overlooked the harbor. I pulled my eyes away remembering the stories the kids told. They said Old Coot spied on people through that dusty window. I held my breath, and inched along her pathway.

I was about to toss the package on her back step, when the door flew open. I stood frozen to one side as I watched Miss Cogshell, in a massive, flowered housecoat, burst through to the yard.

"Oh my, I've lost it." Her eyes darted about at the distant pine trees. Her cobwebby hair, whiter than spray off the crest of a wave, was swept back in a loose bun, and I watched her glasses slip down her bulbous nose. Then she saw me standing there with my mouth open. I was surprised to see a slight flush spread over her large, pale features as she pushed her glasses back up. Never being this close to her before, I was mesmerized by her size.

"I just saw my first spring robin go by the kitchen window," explained Miss Cogshell, in an unexpectedly high, joyful voice. "Sometimes they perch over there on the clothesline."

I glanced at the empty clothesline, and then forced myself to push the mail towards the old woman.

"Oh, my letters. Just let me wash this flour off my hands." She gripped the handrail for support, fumbled with the latch, and then turned her bulky frame back towards me. "Do come in."

Still holding the envelopes, I wanted to say no, but my mouth was too dry. As she opened the door, a sweet smell escaped from within.

"I haven't baked in months. I bake today and here you are—a visitor." Miss Cogshell continued to hold the door, her stretched-out arm like a loaf of freshly risen bread dough. Before I could come to my senses, I stepped inside.

"Now you look familiar. Which one are you?"

"Amy Henderson," I whispered. Miss Cogshell hunched over, peered right into my face, and read my lips through her thick glasses. She looked enormous in her tiny kitchen. And I have to admit I suddenly *felt* like a shrimp.

"Ah, yes, you're in that lovely home on the hill. Your father's done well for himself." Miss Cogshell hauled her massive bulk to the sink, turned on the faucet, and spoke softly, almost as if she'd forgotten I was there. "If only Rosie was here to see. She was always so proud of her boy." Miss Cogshell continued to reminisce while she washed her swollen hands. "There are so many new people from away now. Especially the summer people. Every year someone seems to be coming or going. And busy! My goodness, aren't people busy nowadays?" She stopped and looked at me, her face flushing again. "My land, how I do run on."

I wondered how Miss Cogshell kept track of so much, until I remembered the widow's walk and a chill raced through me. I didn't know what else to do, so again I thrust the bundle of mail towards her.

"Oh, yes, my mail. I do thank you." She wiped her hands dry on a clean dishtowel. Then her face saddened as she took the envelopes. "I have been so self-involved the last few weeks it must've slipped my mind." She glanced through the pile while I edged back towards the door. "Looks like someone cares about this old coot after all."

Did she say *old coot?* My jaw must have dropped a mile, but Miss Cogshell was too busy ripping into her letter from France to notice. She grinned at the rainbow stationery and then put it back on top of the bundle.

"I'll leave these until later. Right now I've got to get you some cookies to bring home to your family." She reached over a row of cookbooks, got down a flowered china plate and gently stacked it with hot gingersnaps.

I fidgeted with my zipper pull while I waited, suddenly needing to go to the bathroom, yet too afraid to ask. My eyes wandered around the cluttered kitchen. A heap of newspapers was stacked next to a curio cabinet, and countertops were layered with odds and ends; only the stove shone spotless. An open cupboard revealed piles of packaged junk food—chips, Twinkies, Devil Dogs. Several faded calendars were tacked to the wall, and hanging in the window was half an old bleach bottle with ivy spilling out of it. Little cups with green sprouts sat in a row on the windowsill.

"Lupines," she explained, catching my glance. "I'll get those into the ground in the next month or so, God willin'."

Finally, she had the plate ready. "You've got your Grandma Rosalie's eyes, you know."

"Thank you," I murmured, as I balanced the plate on top of my mail and pushed out through the back door. That wasn't so bad, I decided.

I had happy memories of Gram Rosalie and could still taste her blueberry pies. Nancy and I spent many mornings picking berries and then Gram would help us turn them into fancy pastry. I'd always make a special mini one in a tiny tin. Just the plumpest, bluest berries would go into my pie and every fork press along the edge of the crust would be as perfect as I could make them.

I tried to picture Gram's eyes. I was only nine when she died but, yes, I was sure they were blue, not brown, so the old lady was evidently crazy.

With a great sigh of relief to have made my escape with all my body parts intact, I hurried for home.

3

I SPENT THE whole of Sunday practicing for an oral report due first period on Monday. I must have gone over the darn thing fifty times in front of my mirror. Didn't matter. The idea of talking while the whole class stared, terrified me. I got no sleep that night.

The next morning at breakfast I couldn't eat. "I feel gross. Maybe I should stay home today."

"What about your report?" My father cut his toast into little squares. "The one about Amelia Earhart?"

Ugh. Even though my dad had a thousand things on his mind, I guess it would be asking too much for him to forget hauling me all the way to the library in Thomaston the previous Saturday to get the book.

"Are you chicken?" Nancy sat across from me, wolfing down Alpha-bits.

"Nope, I forgot all about book reports being due today," I lied.

❧ ❧ ❧

NEEDLESS TO SAY, the long bus ride to school felt more nauseating than usual.

In English class, when our teacher, Mr. Hendricks, asked Craig Miller to start us off, Craig said, "Huh?"

"You were supposed to prepare a three minute talk about a nonfiction book you read." Mr. Hendricks put both hands on his hips, which always left chalky prints on his pants.

"Oh, sure. Of course." Craig swaggered up to the front of the room in his old army jacket. "I read this really cool book about Bonnie and Clyde."

"Really?" Mr. Hendricks raised his eyebrows. "And the book title is?"

Without missing a beat, Craig said, "*The Outlaws*." I could tell Craig hadn't even thought about the assignment until this moment. My mouth fell open as he described a movie I had watched on TV last week. Obviously, he had, too. He wrapped up his speech with "If you want to know how it ends, you'll have to read the book." And then he was back in his seat, grinning.

Mr. Hendricks nodded, oblivious. Gee, that was an easy grade. Too bad for Craig that all his papers couldn't be done out loud.

When it was my turn I shakily moved to the front of the class. I looked out at the faces before me. After a moment I opened my mouth and an odd squeak came out. I heard Pamela snort, followed by Claire's high-pitched giggle. Everything I practiced went poof. I couldn't even remember the title of my book; never mind what happened or what I liked about it. A cottony feeling filled my throat and hotness swept over me. I glanced at my index cards. I had spent hours fiddling with sentences so I could get my whole speech to fit on five cards in tiny print. The words blurred before me.

Mr. Hendricks looked at his watch. "Have you prepared something, Miss Henderson?"

I tried to nod.

"Why don't you sit down then if you have nothing to share?"

In my haste to leave, my hands fell open and index cards flew everywhere. One slid under a boy's sneaker. Down on my hands and knees, I almost had it, but at the last second, the foot slid it farther away. I heard a snicker. I made another grab for the card and got hold of it. The sneaker pressed down on top of it and I don't know what possessed me, but I balled my other hand into a fist and slammed down hard on the kid's toes.

"Ow!" he hollered.

I got my cards all accounted for, banged my head coming up from under the desk, and somehow, with all the power I could summon, placed one foot in front of the other and took the six steps to my desk. I wanted to cry. What a failure.

On my way out of class, Mr. Hendricks told me I could pass in a paper report for a D. One little D wouldn't do too much damage to the super high grades I had in that class, so by the time I rode the bus home, it was a distant memory—one I was glad to be done with.

From the bus window, I glanced down the road to Miss Cogshell's house and saw her come stumbling out the back door again. She must have spotted another robin.

"Old Coot, Old Coot," called the boys' voices from the rear of the bus. I cringed and hoped Miss Cogshell wouldn't hear. She wasn't awful enough to deserve *this*. I peeked around my seat and watched the back of Craig Miller's blond head, unable to tell whether he joined in on the taunts.

Oh well, it wasn't my problem. Even if Miss Cogshell did make delicious cookies, I had to admit I'd rather them tease her than me. That's when I remembered the china plate. My mother had refilled it with some store-bought peppermints, and insisted that the plate be returned by today.

So, later that afternoon, I found myself making my way back down to the pier. When I got to the bottom of our hill, I balanced the plate with two hands and began to walk in as straight a line as I could, one heel coming down right in front of the toes of my other foot. Sometimes I pretended I was on a tightrope and other times I liked to count how many steps it took to get across the road.

Someone's whistling interrupted my silence. I scanned the area and spotted light hair above army green—Craig coming towards the pier on his bike. I'd seen him down here several times lately and wondered what he was up to. I stopped walking like a goober and hid the plate to one side of me. All I needed was to have Craig see me delivering treats to Old Coot. He flew by, however, whistling away, without even noticing me. I moved on towards Miss Cogshell's back door.

I opened the outside glass door and knocked, then waited, and then knocked again. I studied the peeling paint of the buoys that hung on either side of the door. They were blue with two thin green stripes around the bottoms. Fishermen always have their own combination of buoy colors so their markers will be easy to identify. Had Miss Cogshell's father been a fisherman? It was hard to picture her being a little kid with parents and all.

I peered around a tall, bare lilac bush to inspect her backyard. Past the clothesline, in a far corner of the yard was the neatest little shack. A woodshed, I guessed, probably empty now except for passing squirrels. Old tarpaper covered parts of the roof while overgrown shrubbery almost blocked the entrance. A smaller shed across from it must have been an old outhouse.

I turned back and gave one last hard thump, when suddenly the door swung open.

"Miss Cogshell?" I called, as I stepped inside. The house was silent except for the distant ticking of a clock. The deserted kitchen had a surprisingly lived in, cozy feeling. I placed the plate of peppermints on the center checks of the blue vinyl tablecloth, so Miss Cogshell couldn't miss them.

As I turned to leave, my eye caught the sunlight shining in on the corner curio cabinet. The glass doors gleamed and all the little china animals on the shelves came alive. Their many reflections bounced off the mirrors that lined the inside walls of the cupboard. I gazed in at the glimmering figures—turtles, pigs, cats, and even a wolf. A small moose peeked out from behind a plump owl. I stood on tiptoe to see better, but could still only glimpse the head and one antler.

Ever since I'd seen a moose amble through our back yard, I'd been crazy about them. Without thinking, I opened the glass door and reached in behind the owl to pick up the moose. I cradled its smooth finish, more polished than a sea-worn pebble, gently against the palm of my hand.

"You are so cute!" I studied the tiny antlers and grinned at the funny expression on the moose's face. "Now I'll put you back where you belong."

Before I could, I heard Miss Cogshell's heavy footsteps crunching up the gravel of the walkway. I slammed the cabinet door shut, forgetting about the moose. It slipped from my hand and fell on the tile floor, one antler breaking off. I sank to my knees and gathered up the pieces, and then shoved them into my parka pocket, just as Miss Cogshell came in through the door with a grocery bag in one hand and her cane in the other.

My face grew hot as I watched Miss Cogshell discover me with a puzzled look. She placed her bundle on the table using it for support as she inhaled deeply. Then her face brightened. "Returning my plate?"

I nodded.

Faded blue eyes sparkled behind her glasses. "You are like a ray of sunshine in that yellow jacket."

She looked down at her wooden cane, which I now could see was topped with a carved turtle. Its shell made a solid resting place for her hand and its head popped out the front, sporting a whimsical smile. "I don't believe you've met Clyde. Clyde, this is Amy."

I smiled slightly at the turtle. Even though it weighed nothing, the moose felt like the Hope diamond in my pocket. With all my strength I kept my eyes from traveling over to the cabinet. She mustn't notice her moose was gone until I could somehow repair and return it. Until then I felt certain I could be the next thing broken into pieces. Between a bombed oral report and now a smashed, stolen moose, I'd had enough of this lousy day. I whispered that I had to hurry home, waved goodbye, and ran out the back door.

4

WHEN I GOT to the road, there was Craig Miller again. Did he see me run out of Old Coot's house? He had a serious expression on his face as he hurried across the field. For once he wasn't wearing his army jacket, but instead carried it. The coat was wrapped around a log-shaped thing, and I could tell he struggled under the weight of it. As usual, my curiosity got the better of me. What was he doing? It must be important since he left his bike back at the pier. I continued to wonder what he lugged, until he was out of sight. It helped keep my mind off the broken figurine.

By the time I got home my stomach was in knots. I dug into my pocket and pulled out the pieces of the little moose. "I will have to glue you and then somehow sneak you back into the cabinet." I shook my head and wondered how I had managed to get myself into such a mess.

I figured Nancy would comment if I went to bed early, so I waited around while she waltzed across the kitchen linoleum with a towel wrapped round her head. A strip of transparent tape held down her damp bangs. The towel turban made her look extra tall, although even without it, nobody would ever call her a shrimp. Everybody in our family had height except me. Our tall parents were watching TV in the living room.

Every two seconds Nancy would dance over and flip the radio dial back and forth until she found a good song. When my favorite, "Tie a Yellow Ribbon Round the Old Oak Tree," came on, I could barely hear it. That's how loud she sang into her microphone/shampoo bottle, eyes closed, hips swaying. Ever since she fell in love with that kid on *The Partridge Family*, she thought she was some sort of superstar just waiting to be discovered.

I munched on potato chips and pretended to study my math book so she wouldn't notice me. Didn't matter. When her performance ended she wanted to discuss me anyway.

"When's the last time *you* had a shampoo?" she asked in a sickeningly sweet voice.

"Why?"

"Oh, I don't know. You've probably noticed your hair's starting to get a stringy look. I wouldn't worry about it. Probably just needs to be cleaner."

That did it. I had just washed my hair that morning. It wasn't my fault Nancy got the good hair genes. I crumpled up the chip bag, stomped out of the kitchen and went to my room. Why did Nancy have to be so snotty? We used to play together and even sometimes dressed alike when we were little. The last time she said she'd do something with me, I spent twenty minutes arranging Monopoly money while I waited for her to get off the phone. When she finally hung up, she told me she didn't want to play anymore. Guess who had to pack up the game?

The main difference between my sister and me is that she's an outer person and I'm an inner. And I'm not talking about belly buttons. If we both ate a whole box of chocolates, we'd both be bummed out—her because she might look fat. Me? I'd be having ten fits worrying that my arteries might plug up.

I usually felt better in my room, sitting in the nook of my big curved window seat. Every pillow I could find was stuffed into that space and in my opinion it was the only comfortable spot in the whole house. Some of the rooms were so neat and bare they actually echoed. Mom couldn't stand disorder, so no one was allowed to leave stuff lying around. Good thing nobody ever thought to check under my bed.

To me, the only house I'd ever known was rather big and not too cozy. But it was still home and I loved it. How could Nancy ever want to leave? I didn't even like going away for a weekend.

As with most things in life, I liked everything to stay the same. Well, except for one thing. It sure would've been nice to have a town library. When you were a loner, you ended up reading the same books over and over. I think I must have read all fifteen of my Trixie Belden mystery stories about fifty times.

I could spend hours on that window seat looking out into the back woods. The real moose never returned, although I continued to search for him. Seemed everyone in my family had a long list of moose sightings. Everyone but me. But on lucky days, spotted from my window perch, a deer or fox would pass through on silent hooves or paws, unaware of my interest.

While I tried to concentrate on gluing the china moose, my reflection in the mirror on the back of the bedroom door caught my eye. I moved up close to it. Nancy was right—as usual—my hair *was* getting stringier. I'd been so busy counting zits I hadn't noticed. Maybe I'd just start wearing a bag over my head and make everyone happy.

The glue worked well. By morning it was dry and if you squinted your eyes it was hard to see where the moose had been fixed.

~ ~ ~

ONCE AGAIN, AFTER school, I headed towards Miss Cogshell's house. My knees felt like Jell-O every time I thought about how to return the moose. Please let her not be home and let the door be unlocked again. I looked all around before I turned into her walkway. No one in sight.

"This pathway is getting a little too familiar," I grumbled. I knocked. No answer. Thank goodness. I reached for the knob. Just as I did—the door creaked open with Miss Cogshell's welcoming smile behind it.

"Why Amy, what a delightful surprise. I hope you will stay longer this time. I just loved the peppermints. Of course that doctor I visited years ago would be having a conniption if he knew about all these sweets. But as I always say, I was born plump, so I might as well leave this good earth the way I came into it."

As Miss Cogshell chattered on, my face felt like a toasted marshmallow. What in the world was I doing sneaking around like a thief? Finally, I couldn't stand the guilt any longer.

"Miss Cogshell," I interrupted. "I broke your moose." I held it out, stared at the floor, and hoped her smile wouldn't change to anger. My stringy hair hung over my eyes. I bit into my lip as I felt Miss Cogshell lift the moose from my hand, and then heard the slight clink as she placed it on the kitchen table. The silence dragged on as I stood there shaking. I had to do something fast before I became a smooshed bug beneath her giant paw.

"I'm sorry," I spluttered. "The sunlight was shining on your cabinet, and it was so beautiful I couldn't control myself. I had to see the small moose behind the owl because—well, because I really like moose. When I heard you coming, I shut the cabinet and the moose fell and broke." I sniffed loudly. "I glued it."

I peeked up through my hair. "I wanted to sneak it back." I dragged my sleeve across my face and tried to pull myself together. Miss Cogshell stood silent. My temples began to throb. I counted the cuckoos coming from a clock in another room.

Then, before I could grasp what was happening, Miss Cogshell's enormous arms surrounded me in a hug. They even smelled like bread dough, I thought, just before I wondered if I'd be smothered. Not having been hugged since I was a little kid, my emotions must have got all messed up. Next thing I knew, I had pulled away and nearly burst into tears.

"You are an honest young lady," said Miss Cogshell, as she picked up the moose. I could feel her watching me. "I want you to have this moose to remind you of that honesty." Miss Cogshell put the moose into my hand. I held it, and wondered what had just taken place. It wasn't like me to cry or to talk so much.

"Sometime, Amy, maybe—that is, if you visit again—I'll tell you all the stories of these little china animals." She pushed back a wisp of white hair that had escaped her bun as she bent to gaze at the animals with fondness. "They come from all over the world. Some children would not appreciate that sort of thing, but I can tell, you and I are two of a kind." I watched her face with its strong features as she spoke, and realized she wasn't that ugly after all.

As I got ready to leave, I wondered about this and then suddenly thought of something else. "Miss Cogshell, you said I had my grandmother's eyes."

"You do."

"But . . . "

"Not the color, the intensity. Whenever something was bothering Rosie, or she was getting ready to ask an important question, her eyes would blaze like the dickens. Then just as quickly, they would settle back down into peaceful pools."

I smiled as I left the little house once again. This time I didn't bother to check whether anyone was watching.

As I reached the dock, the empty horizon caught my eye. Where were the boats today? Strolling out to the end of the pier, I pulled my parka tight against the strong breeze. I sat down and dangled my feet over the water, startling a seagull that was perched just below. Its cry cut through the silence as it flew out over the rough churning whitecaps and melted into the distance. The crisp salt air refreshed me. I watched a stout man climb into his moored boat, wind up fish line, stack some lobster traps, and then spit into the water. He undid the ropes and started his engine. My eyes followed the boat putt-putt-putting until it was out of sight. I was still gazing out over the icy water when I heard the creaking of the dock boards behind me.

5

"HEY, SHRIMP, WHATCHA lookin' for?" I spun around to find Craig Miller coming towards me. I noticed his bike lying in the dirt just before the pier. Why did he always have to catch me moping around by myself? Miss Unpopular.

"Just looking," I answered, turning back to the ocean. We both remained silent for a minute while I tried to remember how many zits I had counted that morning.

"Bet you'd love to spot a harbor seal." Craig pushed a hand through his wish-I-had-it thick, blond hair. His bangs hung down in his eyes, so he was constantly shoving them out of the way. I suppose it would have been too easy to get a haircut.

I tilted my head up to see him. "Isn't it too cold for them?" My teeth began to chatter, one of those stupid things I do when I'm nervous. I was glad he would think it was only the chilly air.

"Nah, they're year round. They just swim around under the water and pop up through a hole once in a while. If it's frozen solid they swim towards deeper water." Craig stuffed his hands into the pockets of his army jacket as he scanned the horizon. His big ocean-colored eyes squinted in the sun. "There's plenty of fish out there, and so long as a shark doesn't get 'em, they do okay."

Craig was probably the least studious kid in our class, so I was surprised he knew so much about seals and even more amazed that he was actually talking to me. Half the time he wasn't in school. Just the week before, because he couldn't manage to get a permission slip signed, he had to stay alone in the principal's office while we all went on a field trip to a paper mill. Boy, was that a smelly place. Almost as bad as last year's trip to the sardine factory. I shifted uncomfortably as I felt him studying me.

"Can ya keep a secret?" asked Craig with one eyebrow arched.

I nodded.

"Ya swear?"

I nodded again.

"I found an abandoned seal pup yesterday."

Now it was my turn to raise my eyebrows. Was he pulling my leg?

"I'm just checking to make sure his mom isn't looking for him," Craig continued.

"How . . . where?"

"It was lying right by the edge of the shore over there." Craig pointed. "He's got a chewed up flipper that has to heal." Craig looked out over the ocean again, then shook his head. "He would've starved out there. Fed him some herring mashed with milk, 'cause he's not into whole fish yet. Problem is, it's illegal to keep a harbor seal."

"Illegal?"

"Last year they made that Marine Mammal Protection Act. Only Federal agents are allowed to handle harbor seals."

"Where is he?" I asked.

"In my garage. I filled up my kid sister's wading pool and made a ramp for him." Craig's excitement darkened. "My old lady says I've gotta get rid of him though." His rare seriousness faded as quickly as it came. He raised one eyebrow and wrinkled up his nose. "Wanna see him?"

"Yes," I answered without thinking.

"Pup's a little shy of people. That's the other reason I'm not letting the schmucks from school know. But you and him would probably get along okay." He studied me a second. "Stop by after school tomorrow." Craig picked up an old shell, skimmed it across the water and then turned towards shore.

He swung his bike around and called out, "Gotta split," as he leaped on, popped a wheelie and took off.

I'm sure he thought he was pretty cool, but I was thinking he looked kind of goofy. His long legs had outgrown the bike years before.

I watched him ride past Miss Cogshell's, then past the general store and post office until he was out of sight. Right away I started worrywarting about going to his place. I worried that Craig had already changed his mind; that he wished he'd never bumped into me. He'd be embarrassed in front of all his friends if *I* followed him home. On and on my mind circled.

Dad always said that all I needed was a little self-assurance. Easier said than done. Sometimes I wished I could just go to the doctor's and get a shot of confidence. I took one last look at the ocean and trudged up the hill.

That night, I tried to empty my mind by watching *The Waltons* on TV, but instead of thinking about John Boy, I was thinking of Craig. When I remembered how he had teased me about my fuzzy hat in third grade, I decided not to go to his house, but then I kept wondering what Pup was like. It *was* kind of sweet that Craig had already named the seal. Other seal sightings had always been further along the coast in a secluded cove surrounded by steep ledges. Tomorrow might be my only chance to meet a harbor seal up close.

THE NEXT DAY at school, I couldn't concentrate. I really wanted to meet Pup. I glanced over at Craig once during lunch, but he was laughing with the other boys and looking like the same hunk as always. As usual, he wore that big, old army jacket. Did he ever take that thing off? His faded blue-jean legs stretched halfway out into the aisle. With no trouble at all, I worked myself into a frenzy. Had I dreamed up the whole story? Was Craig thinking about Pup, too? Did he hope I would forget to visit? Or maybe he forgot he invited me?

On the bus ride home, I couldn't decide if I should get off the bus one stop early or not. I did.

I watched the bus rumble away as I fanned the fumes from my face, then turned to see Craig waiting at the corner. "C'mon, slow poke," he called. I caught up to him, and we walked together, my short legs taking two steps to each of his long strides.

"Got any pets?" he asked.

I shook my head. For months I had been begging for a pet, and was just beginning to realize it wasn't going to happen. "The last thing we need," my mother had said while she arranged her knick-knacks, "is a dog leaping around or a cat leaving fur balls all over the place." My father would just get that look in his eyes of not quite listening, although once he did shake his head and mumble, "Too much work." They didn't seem to get that I'd be the one taking care of the pet.

"Huh?" he said, leaning down to hear me.

"No, but I want one."

"Me, too. I've always wanted a dog, and now I've got Pup. I know, I know . . . a funny-looking dog but wait 'till you hear him bark." Craig lifted his chin to the sky. "Arf, Arf." He laughed, his head thrown back, white teeth showing. "Just kidding. I'm not sure if he can bark. I think it's only sea lions that do that."

We continued walking in silence while I struggled to think of something to say. The afternoon sun was stronger now, and the wind had died down. I carried my math and social studies books. Craig just had a saggy gym bag. The walk seemed to take forever, and since Port Wells is such a small town, I wondered why I had never bothered to come over this way before.

"You don't talk much, do you?" he said easily, interrupting my thoughts.

I shrugged my shoulders like an idiot. I mean, what was I supposed to say? A few years back my family used to call me chatterbox, but I knew he wouldn't believe that, so why bother getting into it. With Nancy always picking on me, I'd learned it was safer to keep my mouth shut, even at home. I rearranged the books in my arm.

"Hey, I'm not makin' fun of you." Craig grinned. "It just makes big mouths like me want to know what goes on inside your head. That's probably why you're so smart in school. You listen more careful to stuff."

I shrugged again, anxious to change the subject. "So, where's your house?"

"Straight ahead."

Craig lived on a busy street—at least busy for Port Wells—with similar rundown houses along both sides. Each home had a small square of grass between it and the road. I guess he noticed me looking around because he said, "A little different from your mansion."

I was about to tell a white lie and say his place was nice, but Craig put one finger to his lips as though we weren't supposed to be there.

Outside Craig's garage was a big heap of bicycles, tricycles, a wagon, and a lawnmower. I remembered that Craig had several little brothers and sisters.

"Had to make room for Pup," he said.

Craig tossed his gym bag down and grabbed the handle of the garage door, sliding it up. Then he stepped inside, reached into a rusty cooler and pulled out a small fish. Sunshine poured in through the open door. I searched the garage. Craig got down on his knees and motioned for me to do the same.

"Here, Pup," he called quietly. He wiggled the fish out in front of him, and directed his actions toward one area. I peered into the darkened corner and made out two bright eyes above a pair of whiskers, as Pup inched his blubbery shape along the floor. The sunlight bounced off his spotted gray fur. "I think the door scared him," whispered Craig.

"He's beautiful," I said, moving closer. "Why—he's crying!"

Craig grinned. "Nah, seals just make salt tears whenever they're out of the water."

We watched him for a while. Pup didn't want the fish, but he did go for a swim in the little pool. His sleek body floated in the shallow water. He dragged the poor wounded flipper behind him. Pup swam in a few circles. There wasn't room to do much more.

"He needs to be set free as soon as he heals but it may take a few weeks. I'll miss him."

I glanced at Craig as he watched Pup slide up and over the edge of the pool. Was this really the wild, joking kid who called me Shrimp?

Craig went back to tempting Pup with the fish, but Pup appeared content to lie on the dry cement in a patch of afternoon sun.

"C'mon, Pup," coaxed Craig. He brought the fish right over to the little seal and was dangling it in front of his nose, when all of a sudden, Pup tossed his head high and let out a loud snort of disgust. It startled Craig so much that he stumbled back and fell into the pool.

I rushed over. I wondered whether it would be silly to offer to help Craig climb out of the tiny pool. He jumped up quick, looking like a big sloppy seal himself. His blue jeans were dripping wet, and he still clutched the little fish. I tried like anything to keep a straight face.

"I guess he doesn't want this," said Craig, tossing the fish back into the cooler. "Hey—what are you . . . hey, are you laughing at me?"

Craig looked me straight in the eye, and I don't know what my problem was, maybe just nerves, but next thing I knew I burst into giggles and couldn't stop. We both laughed until I got a pain in my side. Pup watched us with what I decided was an amused expression.

Then the door that led from the garage to the house swung open, and I watched Craig's face change to anger or fear—I wasn't sure which. It took me by surprise. Craig's mother stood in the doorway with an odd look on her face. She was a pretty woman, like someone you might see on TV, except there was something sad about her.

"Time we split this scene," said Craig, almost shoving me back out of the garage. His mother watched us through narrowed eyes. Her cheeks were flushed, and as she stepped into the garage she stumbled a bit on the stairs.

"That—animal—has—got—to—go." She spoke sharply, and paused between each word. "You're supposed to be helping me with the babies after school."

"Right, Ma." Craig pulled down the garage door. He mumbled a few swears under his breath.

I grabbed my books and raced down the driveway to catch up to him.

As we reached the street, Craig's front door crashed open. "It has to be gone by tomorrow," his mother screamed after us.

Embarrassed, I snuck a look at Craig. His face was distorted with emotion.

"Now you've met Super Mom," he said too loud, attempting to laugh.

"She probably just had a rough day." I ran a few more steps to keep up. "Don't you want to change your wet clothes?"

"I don't wanna go back there. The sun will dry 'em." Craig jerked his hair back out of his eyes and looked at me. "She's like that every day. And if I don't find a place for Pup, fast, I'll have to throw him back in the ocean tomorrow."

"Maybe my house," I offered.

"Isn't your dad good pals with the harbormaster?"

"Oh, yeah." How in the world would Craig know this? "You're right, he is. I can't figure it out. Howard is so stern-looking, yet half the town seems to think he's wonderful."

"Ha," said Craig. "That's because half the town is hoping ol' Howie will overlook their little crimes."

"Maybe he could help?"

"No way. Howie's not finding out. And it would take forever for those Federal guys to get here. That time the Percys had questions about their blue lobster, it took them a stinkin' week to show up." Craig lifted and shook his legs, one at a time, in an attempt to dry them faster, then glanced at me.

"So let me make sure I've got this straight," I said, looking down. "You're breaking the law and could get arrested."

"If you wanna think of it that way. I think of it as saving Pup's life." Craig looked straight into my eyes again. "Would you have left Pup to die?"

I glanced away, those blue eyes making me nervous, and thought some more. My dad was always talking with his friend Howard. He was part of the little group my parents got together with. Mom enjoyed having fancy dinner parties while I hid up in my room, bored out of my brain, munching junk food. No, they wouldn't feel right keeping information from Howard. And from what I'd heard, Howard went straight by the book. If there was something wrong going on, no matter how trivial, he took after it like it was a mass murder. Regardless, now that I'd met Pup, I had to help save him.

6

WE CONTINUED WALKING towards the pier while Craig and I went back and forth discussing everyone who lived in the Port. No place seemed right for an illegal seal.

And then I thought of the perfect location. Would a house filled with tiny china animals, including a few marine species, have room for a real one?

"I know who might help us."

"Great," said Craig. "Who?"

I took a deep breath and said, "Miss Cogshell."

Craig widened his eyes and then broke into that grin of his.

"You've gotta be kidding. Old Coot? She'd probably brew him in a pot."

"I used to feel that way, but she's okay once you get to know her."

"Nah." Craig shook his head like I was crazy, then jerked his bangs up. "Do you?"

"Do I what?"

"Know her?" Craig's voice impatient.

"Oh, well, um . . . not really." I looked down at my sneakers. Maybe someday I'd be brave enough to answer those kind of questions with, "Sure. Want to make something of it?" Then again, Miss Cogshell could hate real animals for all I knew. There weren't even any cats around her place. Maybe she was allergic. I was standing there feeling crummy when an even better idea hit me.

"I've got it. Down behind her house there's an old woodshed. Real private."

"I've seen it." Craig nodded, turning to go. "I'll get him in there tonight."

"What about me?" I asked.

"I'm doing it around midnight," he tossed over his shoulder. "A little past your bedtime, Shrimp."

I watched him go up the road in his soggy jeans, and wondered what his problem was. If he could get out at midnight, so could I. Besides, it was my idea to use the woodshed.

That night, after filling three pages of my diary, I stretched out on top of my bed, fully dressed, my alarm set for 11:30 p.m. I figured I could get a little sleep. Wrong. Instead I tossed and turned, glancing at the glowing dial of my clock radio, for what seemed like hours.

After I finally drifted off, soft music woke me with a start. I dove over and turned off "Crocodile Rock" before the sound could reach my sleeping family. Grabbing a flashlight and my sneakers, I listened to Nancy's snoring for a moment at her door. Then I tiptoed down the stairs, stretching over the creaky third step.

Once outside, I slipped into my sneakers. Racing down the hill under the dark pines gave me the creeps, but once I broke through to the road, I saw it was almost a full moon and quite bright. My heart jumped into my throat when a rabbit darted across the road.

For courage, I began talking out loud. "Well, at least it's small. Better than a humongous moose at this hour." Then I told myself sternly, "Yikes, don't think about that." This was the one time I'd rather *not* bump into a moose, no matter how much I loved them. I hurried past Miss Cogshell's shadowy house, then the store, post office, and other dark houses until I reached Craig's.

His garage door was just inching up with him on the inside, his beat-up sneakers showed below. This would take a while. He was obviously trying to be as quiet as possible. I looked around, spotted a little red wagon, and carried it silently to the top of the driveway by the garage. By then I could see Craig up to his shoulders.

"Hi," I whispered.

"Wha . . . ?" The garage door slipped a few inches, then Craig's face peered out from beneath it. "Here, hold this," he whispered back, acting like I didn't just scare the living daylights out of him. I reached up and held the door in place while Craig moved in to get Pup, now a blanket-covered lump. He plopped him into the wagon. I inched the heavy door down.

At the last minute, Craig wiggled back under to grab the pool, tugging at it, then lifting to let the water splash down the driveway.

"You can pull the wagon, I'll lug this." He swung the small plastic pool up over one shoulder.

I didn't say anything, just started pulling that wagon, feeling Craig was lucky I'd come along. He hadn't even thought to bring a flashlight. Pup squirmed under the blanket for a while, and then settled down. The squeaking of the wagon wheels was the only sound as we moved along the gritty road.

In fact, the wagon made so much noise, we didn't hear the one-eyed pick-up truck barreling along until it was almost on top of us. Its lone headlight lit up our miniature convoy.

"Stop, Craig!" I bent over to block Pup. The truck slowed down and the pale face of Sally Johnson's husband peered out through the dirty window. He looked right at Pup who had somehow wiggled more than his nose out from beneath the blanket. Uh oh. My chest pounded and my breath came in quick huffs. The engine rumbled while Ed Johnson studied the scene. I lowered my head and let my hair hide my face. Would he report us?

However, to my surprise, the old Ford sped up again, and left a trail of dust in its wake. Whew. I guess he thought it was normal for two kids to be out at midnight, pulling a baby seal in a little red wagon.

"Good thing he doesn't have his wife's nose for gossip," I mumbled, as I gave Pup an extra pat before I tucked him back under the blanket.

"Are you kiddin'?" Craig laughed. "Ed's the one should be worried. Where's he coming from at this hour, driving so wild?"

We started moving towards the pier again, faster than before. In the far distance, the lighthouse periodically shot a faint flicker of light over the dark water. Now that I wasn't alone, I realized how incredibly beautiful late night could be.

After a left turn before Miss Cogshell's house, we groped our way through the trees to the woodshed. I used my flashlight to watch for rocks and sticks that might upset our precious load.

Shoving shrubs aside, I aimed my light high on the old padlock, so Craig could yank it off and open the heavy woodshed door, its rusty hinges too loud for this quiet night. We both grimaced, and for a second we held onto the door, waiting for the house lights to flash on, but the noise must not have been as loud as we imagined. All remained dark.

We squeezed the pool into the woodshed. Then, we lifted Pup out of the wagon, through the door and placed him into the dry pool. There was gray darkness inside, and the moonlight from outside cast strange black shadows on the strewn wood shavings that covered the floor. Craig peered at the rusty tools that lined the workbench, but I had no interest, fearing there would be a zillion spiders. Pup slid about on his plump belly, probably wondering what in the world he was doing there.

"What about water?" I said.

"If there was a jug in here I could fill it at the pier," said Craig. He looked around and shrugged. "Hey, I can't think of everything."

Finally, we gave up and knew we'd have to go find a bucket.

As we were leaving, I turned to look back at Pup in the dull moonlight of the open door. His head was lifted high and cocked to one side; two bright eyes watched us. He didn't know we were about to leave him in a dry pool in the pitch dark. I swallowed hard, and then stepped outside.

Craig pulled the big, wood door shut behind him, and hooked it with the broken padlock. I had just turned my flashlight off and was about to tell Craig I would stay and wait with Pup after all, when the light over Miss Cogshell's back entry came on. Inch by inch, her door creaked open.

"Hello-o," Miss Cogshell called out into the darkness.

I glanced at Craig—silent and staring. I hadn't noticed how cold the night had become. I started to move towards her as she came outside and down the steps, until I felt Craig's hand tighten on my arm.

Moonlight fell on Miss Cogshell's long, loose white hair, and she appeared to be ten feet tall. She gripped her walking stick, and moved a step closer. I held my breath as her giant shadow crept towards us. The cane made a scary silhouette, like she was armed with a dangerous weapon, but then I remembered the handle was only the shape of a turtle named Clyde. My heart still raced and I wondered if Miss Cogshell was frightened, too.

I jerked my arm free of Craig. "It's me, Amy," I called across the yard.

"Oh, thank goodness," she said.

Craig started to bolt.

"Is someone else with you?" she asked.

"Um." I watched Craig disappear into the dark trees, and then turned back to Miss Cogshell. "May I talk with you?"

"Of course, come in. I am very curious to find out why you are crashing around my backyard in the dark." Miss Cogshell went into her house and began turning lights on.

"Come on," I said, looking to where I figured Craig must be standing.

He suddenly whispered, right in my ear. "Are you gonna tell her?"

I sucked in air and turned. "Don't sneak up on me like that."

Craig threw up his hands. "I might as well take Pup home before she reports him."

"Well, we've got to do something."

I finally convinced him to move towards the house, but as we got nearer, Craig hung back a few steps.

"This stinks. Old Coot's gonna ruin the whole thing," he said.

"Trust me. Everything will be okay." I rapped on the glass of the outside door. A moment later Miss Cogshell filled the doorway.

"Amy, what . . . " she stopped. "Why, you *have* brought a friend." I turned and saw Craig gawking up at Miss Cogshell as though he had never seen her before. The tallest kid in school suddenly looked short.

"This is Craig. He's got . . . well, we've got a problem."

"I guess you do," she said. "Come in—even at midnight, there is nothing that can't be solved with cookies." I blinked my eyes in the sudden brightness, then scowled at Craig so he'd follow. You'd think we were Hansel and Gretel at the witch's gingerbread house by the length of time it took him to get into the kitchen.

"There's a baby seal, and he's hurt," I began, as I helped myself to a chocolate chip cookie. I glanced over at Craig, silent for once, who stood with his hands in the pockets of his army jacket. His head was bent as though he read the stack of newspapers beside him. "We thought maybe . . . well, we don't know where to keep him. Craig can't keep him in his garage anymore."

"In his garage! Well, I should say not," said Miss Cogshell. "A garage is no place for a seal." She pushed long, silvery strands back over her shoulder. I had never seen such hair and wondered if all old lady buns held this glory.

Craig looked defiantly at her; his blue eyes blazed. Then he glanced at me with a *told you she wouldn't help us* look.

"There's a legal problem, too," I added, looking straight at Craig, so he'd explain.

"Yeah, there's some law about it," he mumbled, shoving his bangs back. "I just want to keep him 'til his flipper heals."

"A law, you say?" Miss Cogshell scooped up bobby pins from the counter. She twisted a quick ponytail and began to insert the pins into her hair. "Bring him right over," she said at last.

"Really?" I shrieked. "Oh, I knew you'd help us." I, who so recently didn't like hugs, felt like throwing my arms around her, but was too aware of Craig standing an inch away in the tiny kitchen.

Miss Cogshell made a shooing motion with her hands and before she could say scat, we rushed through the door, out to the woodshed. We grabbed Pup, stuffed him back in the wagon and bounced him across the yard, Craig ducking beneath the clothesline.

Miss Cogshell watched for us and flung the door open wide, when we arrived. Her hair was caught up now in the usual bun.

Craig lifted him out of the wagon and the three of us went inside. What would Pup think of his new home? I wondered.

"What a cunnin' little thing you are." Miss Cogshell looked down at Pup's bewhiskered face. "I'll put some nice salt in the tubbie to help your boo-boo." She kept talking baby talk in this high, squeaky voice. I didn't dare look at Craig because I knew he'd be making a face and I'd burst out laughing.

We got Pup settled in the tub, hung around to watch him check out his new pad for a few minutes, and then flew for home.

7

THE NEXT DAY, I stopped by to visit Pup and found Craig hanging around near Miss Cogshell's walkway.

"Aren't you going in?" I asked.

"Of course." Craig shifted his weight from one foot to the other. "I came to see Pup."

After we were inside with Pup and Miss Cogshell, Craig warmed up a bit. Pup was bellying about the linoleum floor, enjoying all the attention. Craig liked to tease him by tickling his nose. Pup gave it right back and once he nipped Craig's finger hard enough to make him wince in pain. Pup licked the wound, and Craig's face softened.

When the cuckoo clock started cuckooing, Craig had to run to the parlor and see what that was all about.

"Hey cool, the bird pops out. Where'd ya get this thing? Looks foreign, like we should be sitting here chewing on slabs of bread covered in goat cheese, or somethin'."

Once Craig got talking, I didn't think he'd ever shut up. Miss Cogshell stood there grinning at him, holding her big sides, so I guess she enjoyed him. She sometimes talked a lot herself; however, when someone else was speaking, she gathered up every word in her deep listening way.

DURING THE WEEKEND, I stopped by to see Miss Cogshell and Pup several times. Craig was there every time, trying to get Pup to eat. I wished there was something I could do to help. Already, Pup looked thinner.

Once in a while when Craig was in the other room with Pup, I'd sit at the kitchen table and help Miss Cogshell with baking or whatever she was up to.

The stories Miss Cogshell told me about the different china animals and how they came into her collection were so interesting that I often didn't notice the growing dusk outside. One of my favorite tales was about her friend from England. Margie had been stranded on an iceberg while on a scientific expedition in Antarctica. After her safe return, she had sent the tiny penguin to Miss Cogshell.

Miss Cogshell chuckled. "Just a little souvenir. But that wee fellow started up quite an assembly now, didn't he?"

ON SUNDAY NIGHT, Craig and I left Miss Cogshell's at the same time. We had stayed later than usual. Darkness spilled misty shadows over the port. The harbormaster's truck passed by as we stepped onto the road.

"We'd better be more careful," I said. "It will look suspicious if we're always coming and going at odd hours."

Craig laughed. "Suspicious?"

"If he gets wind of Pup, he'll be looking out for strange behavior."

"I guess." Craig shoved his hair back. "I'm starving." He dug through his pockets. "Crud, just an empty Charleston Chew."

As he pulled out the candy wrapper, something else landed on the ground by my feet. A cigarette. I scrunched up my nose. "What's with that?"

Craig looked at it a moment as though it were some alien being. "Oh, yeah, I forgot. I took that from Ma's stash about an hour before I found Pup."

"You were going to smoke it?" I asked, making another face.

"Well, guess you could say I considered it, but things are different now." Craig picked up the cigarette and pointed it at me. "Grab the end and make a wish."

I did and then we pulled, so hard I almost fell backwards. It ripped into three pieces. Craig ended up tossing the whole thing into a nearby barrel. "Don't know what I was thinking. Last thing I wanna be is like my old lady."

"Well, I guess we both got our wish then," I said. "The last thing I want is to hang around with someone who smells like an old ashtray." And then I remembered. "Uh oh, I didn't do my math homework."

A wide grin spread across Craig's face as he whispered "slack-er" low and slow, close to my ear.

"I'm not! I always do my work."

"Slaaack-er," he repeated.

Even though I knew I'd just stay up an extra half hour to do the assignment, his teasing made me feel fun, kind of reckless and carefree.

We were moving onto the pier, when the harbor master's truck came back from the other direction, going slow.

"Duck!" said Craig. We leaped off the side of the dock, and landed on the small beach. We shimmied over to a heap of wreckage and kept ourselves low behind it. I could hear the truck stop and the door rattle open.

The wide beam of light from Howard's flashlight swept over, just above our heads—back and forth several times.

"Anybody out there?" Howard called.

My heart thumped. Neither Craig nor I uttered a peep. Through a slit in a slab of driftwood, I watched Howard check his boat locks and then climb back into the truck.

Howard peeled out, his tires burning rubber. Covered in sand from head to toe, I rolled onto my back and started laughing. "What are we hiding for? We don't even have Pup with us!"

"Think of it as a Howie drill," said Craig.

LATER THAT NIGHT, after whipping through my math, I filled four pages of my diary and then found it hard to sleep; that's how excited I was. Spring was halfway over, although the thermometers didn't seem to realize it. Hopefully, warmer weather would soon come. Already I worried about Pup's release back to the ocean. I wanted to keep him forever. All I could think about was Pup and Craig and Miss Cogshell.

~ ~ ~

ON MONDAY, IN the school cafeteria, I noticed Craig with his friends at the next table. The kids who sat at the end of my table had already cleared out, so I sat alone as usual. It seemed to be a silent agreement between Craig and me to act like we didn't even know each other. The other boys at his table jumped up. They shot lunch bags into the barrel and tossed their trays onto the counter. I took small bites out of my cookie and pretended not to notice them.

"Come on, Craig," shouted a kid, "baseball time."

"Catch ya later," mumbled Craig. He sat staring at his half-eaten lunch, both elbows supporting his head. It was rare to see him down.

I stood, popped the last of my cookie into my mouth, took a few steps, and then forced myself to stop by his table. He looked half-asleep under his shag of blond hair.

"You okay?" I asked.

Craig jerked his head up, raised one eyebrow and stifled a yawn. "I'm just thinkin' 'bout Pup," he said. "I spent half the night trying to get him to eat something."

"Half the night?"

"Miss C. left the door open for me. I had to sneak out of my place, then sneak back in again. Something's gotta change." Craig looked down at his sandwich again. "I know a tub's no place for a seal, but if he doesn't learn to eat fish, he'll never survive. He was probably still nursing when I found him. Don't know if I'm doing it wrong or if he's homesick or what."

"Maybe they have a book on it at the library."

He shrugged. "Beats me, but, hey, time is running out."

"True, and who knows when I can convince my father to drive me over to Thomaston. Well, his flipper has been looking better," I offered.

"Yeah, it's getting there. You going over today?"

I nodded, but Craig was taking aim at a breadcrumb. He snapped it with his index finger, to another table. "Well?" he said, turning to stare at me, like he really wanted an answer.

I cleared my throat. "I'll be there."

Craig stretched, dumped his sandwich in the trash, then called back over his shoulder. "See ya later, Shrimp."

I watched him saunter out of the lunchroom. Grrr! Couldn't he see how much I hated the name Shrimp? I guess I'd have to tell him—one of these days. Not realizing air was trapped inside, I clapped my lunch bag flat. The bang was so loud I jumped, then I looked around quick. The last few tables of kids were too busy talking to notice, but the custodian was staring at me with raised eyebrows. I tossed my bag into the barrel, and tried to keep a straight face as I, too, sauntered out of the lunchroom.

~ ~ ~

NO MATTER WHAT kind of day I'd had, there was a certain feeling that came over me the minute I walked into Miss Cogshell's home. I don't know if it was the cooking smells or the soothing tick-tock of the cuckoo clock, or something more. I seemed to have an ability there to think things I had never thought before. As though feelings had been stored deep inside me and were slowly being let out like air from a beach ball. I wasn't sure anymore whether I was helping Miss Cogshell, a lonely old lady, or if she was helping me.

I found Miss Cogshell in a dither hovering over Pup and Craig. "The poor little thing doesn't look too well." She wrung her plump hands.

Pup was lying in the corner of the bathroom tub with the same long face that Craig had worn at lunchtime. A book about whales, dolphins, and seals was on the nearby countertop.

I glanced at Craig in amazement. "How did you get to the library and back so fast?"

"Don't even know how to get to the big city, never mind to the library. This belongs to Miss C. Great pictures, but zippo on feeding." Then Craig turned away and started waving a fish around. "You must be hungry by now, Pup."

"Don't go falling in the tub," I said.

"Ha ha." Craig rolled his eyes, "Why don't you try then?"

I stuck the fish in my jacket pocket, then got on my hands and knees and inched over to Pup. "Hi Pup," I whispered. I had read an article about an orphanage and figured all babies were basically alike when it came to needs. First it's a matter of earning trust. I brought my hand out slowly and patted Pup's satin head, then up and down his long, sleek back. I could feel him relax under my hand. Little by little I slid the bottom of my jacket up over the edge of the tub, while continuing to pat Pup. Craig and Miss Cogshell watched in silence from the hallway.

After a while my hand started going numb from sliding back and forth over the spotted fur. I shifted so Pup's nose lined up in front of my jacket pocket. I kept patting with stiff fingers as I watched Pup's whiskers start to twitch. Pup's dark eyes seemed full of trust as he looked at me. After a few more minutes, Pup stuck his nose right in my pocket and pulled out the fish. I held my breath, and a second later, the fish was gone.

"Alright!" Craig cheered.

Pup stuck his nose back in.

"He wants more." Craig tossed me another fish. I sneaked it into my pocket while Pup wasn't looking. Then I draped my jacket back over the side of the tub, and he went fishing again.

"Good job, Amy," said Miss Cogshell. She gave a long sigh as she pushed her glasses up her nose. "Now that Pup is eating, I guess I'll go into the parlor and relax a while." I watched her squeeze her bulky form around the corner and for the first time wondered exactly how old she was. I felt Craig's eyes on me and glanced over at him.

"I hadn't noticed the heart before," I said.

"Huh?" Craig wrinkled his nose.

"The little heart shape above Pup's left eye." I pointed out the rough spot of white.

Craig leaned way in over my head to see. His jacket smelled like a fresh cut lawn. I held my breath. Then he straightened and shrugged one shoulder. "If you say so. Anyway, I hope Pup'll eat from my pocket, too. You've got the magic touch." Craig gave me his widest smile ever, and I thought I'd melt right on the spot.

"Thanks," I managed to say, shaking the pins and needles out of my hand, as the cuckoo started calling.

"Yikes, I've gotta go." Craig jumped up. "My old lady's really been on my case lately."

"I know what you mean," I agreed. "My mom's been asking where I go every day." I thought about how Mom's face had lit up the first time I mentioned I'd be with a friend. She'd been waiting a long time for me to have friends like Nancy had. But I wasn't ready to share my new adventures with her; not yet.

Craig stared at me while my mind returned to the present. "No, Shrimp." He paused. "You don't know." He headed down the hall and out through the kitchen. The backdoor slammed behind him.

Remembering Craig had been up all night trying to feed Pup, I figured he had a right to get cranky. Pup rolled over onto his back and I rubbed his belly for a few minutes until he looked ready to fall asleep.

I tiptoed into the parlor and found Miss Cogshell dozing in her big chair. It was a comfortable looking chair of soft blue, the fabric worn and faded. A cheery red-checked dish cloth hung over the top of the chair to protect where her snow-white hair pressed gently against its back. Her trusty cane, Clyde, rested at her side. Miss Cogshell's breathing joined the cuckoo clock in a soothing duet. I took the opportunity to study some of her book titles. She had a good collection of Agatha Christie books and I couldn't wait to ask her if I could read one. For now, though, I'd just borrow the book about whales, dolphins, and seals.

A new book in the house—without it following the major ordeal of a trip to the Thomaston Public Library—stood out. So, when I got home, it took Nancy all of three minutes to spot it hanging out of my book bag.

"Hmm, what's this? *Whales, Seals, & Dolphins*?" Nancy flipped it over. "Where'd you get this?"

I grabbed the book from her.

"Ew, touchy today, aren't we? Looks like little Amy's got another report due, everybody."

"Maybe, I do. Mind your own beeswax!" The last thing I needed was for Nancy to question my sudden interest in marine mammals.

8

BETWEEN MATH AND Social Studies, Claire, one of my least favorite people, made a huge deal of passing out party invitations. She pretended to sneak them onto each desk, but those of us who were left out would have to be deaf, dumb, and blind not to have noticed.

I kept my eyes on my book while Pamela Johnson, who'd been crazy about Craig since first grade, and who was my *very* least favorite person, helped out her best friend by delivering one to Craig.

Out of the corner of my eye, I watched him open it. He held the card up for a moment and I could read every word. The invitation said: "A boy-girl party this Saturday at 4!! Pizza, games, and lots of fun!! Be there or be square!!"

Hmm, guess I'd be square then.

❧ ❧ ❧

I SPENT THE rest of the week pretending not to notice or care about Claire's party. There had to be other kids not going, but those who were going made the most noise, until it seemed everyone would be there. I told myself it didn't matter. I mean just because I liked pizza and playing games didn't mean I had anything in common with Claire and Pamela. I wondered what motivated the other kids to go along with the crowd. Or was I kidding myself? Would I, too, have jumped at the chance to go?

I watched Pamela reapply her lipstick for the third time.

No, I decided. I was better off by myself. I just wished it didn't feel so lousy.

ON SATURDAY, CRAIG left Miss Cogshell's house a few hours before me. I figured he was going home to get ready for Claire's party.

"Is everything okay, Amy?" asked Miss Cogshell after he'd left.

I nodded. "Yeah, I'm just tired."

The two of us read our books in the parlor. Like a couple of old biddies, we settled in for a quiet weekend.

Near sunset, I finally said goodbye to Pup and Miss Cogshell, and plodded towards home.

As I neared the wharf I heard faint musical sounds. The low sun was in my eyes, but I could make out someone sitting at the end of the pier and by the stick-shape jutting out, I knew they must be playing a guitar. I moved closer and shaded my eyes. One of my favorite songs reached me and my mouth fell open when I recognized Craig's old army jacket. As he continued to strum, I tiptoed over and sat cross-legged about three feet behind him. To steal the words from another favorite song, I felt like he was singing my life—like he was reading my diary out loud.

Craig sang out about the seasons and how all I had to do is call and he'd be there. He finished up the last verse of "You've Got a Friend," while I sat there dumb-struck. Then I clapped.

"Hey, you shouldn't sneak up on people." Craig threw me his trademark grin.

"That was great! How did you do that? I didn't know you played." I was so excited I couldn't stop babbling. "I've always wanted to play music, but I can't sing. And then in third grade when we had those recorders, I ended up faking it the whole time. I just couldn't keep the beat."

"Well, I don't really play. I mean I don't read music or nothing. One of those big houses out on the main road was getting rid of this a few years ago. I put new strings on it."

"So, you play by ear? And sing, too?"

"I just fool around. Really, it's nothing." Craig looked content as he tuned one of the strings.

"I thought you'd left early to go to Claire's party," I said.

"Nah, I had to watch my little brother while my mom took my sisters over to Thomaston." Craig nodded towards a little boy on the beach, a short distance away. The towheaded boy, a miniature version of Craig, carried a green pail. Every few steps, he stopped to dig through the seaweed, until he found a new treasure for his bucket.

"Wasn't in the mood to play party games anyhow," Craig added.

I felt as happy as a clam at high tide. "Well, your music sounds cool."

Craig laughed. "I know all of three songs, and I mess up a lot."

"Play some more?"

Craig played another song. He used a small flat shell to pluck the strings. Then he passed me the guitar. "Give it a shot."

"I can't."

"Here, position it like this." Craig adjusted the instrument. "Okay, hold these three strings down and strum here." His voice was low and musical as he taught me the chord.

The guitar felt bulky and awkward in my lap. I produced a few twangs. Craig's pale hair hung over his face, and I was grateful he couldn't see me. My face felt the heat of the sunset as he pressed my fingers into place. My breathing quickened. At that moment, it was like I was no longer Amy and would maybe do anything this guy asked. Even jump off the pier in my favorite lime-green sneakers. The feeling scared me, and I quickly handed Craig back his guitar.

"Got to go," I said. I jumped up and got myself a safe distance away. Then I turned and waved. I couldn't stop grinning. I hummed "You've Got a Friend" all the way home. People sure could be surprising.

9

WE ALWAYS GOT progress reports way ahead of report cards so there wouldn't be any surprises. When Mrs. Marston, the homeroom teacher, handed them out, I saw Craig flip his over quick and then slump further down in his seat. My grades were pretty good, but I worried that Craig had spent more time with Pup than with his homework.

We filed out of the room. Those of us who rode the bus got on. As always I sat second seat from the front on the right. Craig moved past me to the back of the bus, the sleeve of his army jacket brushing my shoulder.

As we rumbled along, I listened to all the usual fooling around. I sat up as tall as I could, peeked into the bus driver's rearview mirror and discovered Craig wasn't joining in. He was slouched down, staring out the window.

Unfortunately, Miss Cogshell was walking past the post office when the bus came barreling around the corner.

"Old Coot!" a couple of the usual voices yelled. The familiar words stung my ears like never before.

All of a sudden I heard this wicked loud "Shut up!" I spun around and saw a red-faced Craig standing in the aisle with clenched fists. His friends stared at him with blank faces.

Then one said, "It's okay man, we didn't realize she was your girlfriend."

Another mocking voice called out, "Pamela will be jealous." Pamela, hair teased high, blushed and giggled on cue.

I was waiting for Craig to smack them; luckily we got to his stop right then. Craig grabbed his books, pushed past everyone and got off. That's when I realized I had been holding my breath. I let it out slowly.

WHEN I GOT home, Mom and Dad were reviewing Nancy's progress report.

"Ooh, C+ in Math!" said Mom.

"Nice work, Nance," said Dad. "You brought that grade right back up."

"How did you do, Amy?" asked my mother. A bottle of Windex and a soft cloth stood on the windowsill, ready for her next cleaning project.

"I'm sure she'll make honor roll like always." Nancy spoke with a bored sigh.

"Yep." I handed the details to my mother.

"Hmm," she said, "Math went down to a B."

Dad took off his reading glasses and looked at me. My father was a slim, quiet man with a clean cut look. At times like this he appeared quite scholarly. "Are you having trouble understanding it?" he said.

"Ah . . . *no*. It's a B. Not a D!" I always seemed to get the short end of the stick when it came to daughter compliments.

Nancy pinched her nose. "Something's fishy."

"What do you mean?" asked Dad. "Do you think Amy's grade is in error?"

Nancy sniffed around me until her nose came close to my jacket pocket. "Phew! What I mean is: Amy smells like an old fish!"

Well, *that* changed the subject. I made a mental note to wash my parka and a few minutes later I was on my way to Miss Cogshell's. I was pretty sure that Nancy's grades would be as good as mine if she spent as much time studying as she did writing fan letters to David Cassidy and the rest of the Partridge Family.

❧ ❧ ❧

MISS COGSHELL HAD left the inside door open, probably to let the sun heat up the kitchen through the glass, while she caught up on some more letter writing. I pressed my nose against the door to see better, and she motioned for me to come in.

"Guess what!" I announced as I stepped inside. "We got progress reports today and I'm going to make the honor roll."

She smiled and said, "How wonderful, Amy. Good job! That explains it; Craig must have received his report, too." She nodded her head to indicate he was in with Pup. "When he put his school supplies on the table, a paper slipped out. He crumpled that thing up like it was on fire and tossed it fast."

"Uh oh." I peered over to see the crinkled ball just sitting there in the bucket two feet away.

"Now don't go getting any ideas while I'm busy concentrating on this letter." Miss Cogshell opened a sheet of flowered stationery, her eyes still watching the wastebasket.

Before I knew it I was unwrapping the wrinkled document. Two F's, two D's, two A's, and a C. Something made me look up and there stood Craig in the doorway to the hall. He pushed through the kitchen and out the back door before I could even think.

"A pretty lousy report." I placed it on the table.

"Ayuh." Miss Cogshell shifted her weight in the chair, the floorboards creaking beneath her. "And the poor kid isn't too proud of it. He feels everyone's against him. I don't know how they expect him to get any work done at that crazy house of his. With his father away and his mother loose as a goose. Oh my, I shouldn't be saying all this."

"I'll go find him," I said.

Craig sat at the end of the pier. I plunked myself down beside him. We watched the waves and seagulls for a while. Someone had left a fish mess on the edge of the pier and it didn't take long for a scrawny cat to come sniffing around. A seagull scared him away, but the cat soon circled back to finish his meal.

"Ya know, you could have asked to read my private stuff." Craig jerked his bangs back.

He was right. I felt crummy and attempted to make things better. "I saw a couple of A's on there."

"Yeah, art and gym. You can think what you want, but I don't want your sympathy. And don't ever call me stupid."

"I never called you that. You may have this big complex about where you live, how your parents are, and how much money you have, but . . . "

Craig leaped up. I had never seen him so angry. "Why don't you just go home, Goodie-Two-Shoes, so you won't catch cooties."

I opened my mouth to speak.

"Just get outta my face. Little Miss Try to Fix Everything."

He stomped away down the road. My lip quivered as he faded into a small green dot. Then he disappeared entirely. Two seagulls squabbled over the mess the cat left behind.

I went back to Miss Cogshell's and sat with Pup under the kitchen table while she read in the parlor.

"Maybe I didn't handle that so well?" I said.

Pup snorted in agreement.

THAT NIGHT AT the dinner table everyone talked about problems the Skylab space station was having after its first launch. My head was so full I couldn't follow the conversation. Nancy's elbow practically touched my plate the whole time. I put up with it for at least three minutes and then shoved my half-eaten dinner closer to her.

"Do you have to hog the whole table?" I leaped up and headed for my room. "I'm not hungry, anyway!"

"What's her problem?" said Nancy. "Can I have her dessert?"

I could hear my parents' confused whispers as I ran upstairs.

10

I WOKE EARLY the next morning and discovered I still had on yesterday's clothes. My mouth tasted like an old trout. I rummaged through my bureau until I found a favorite shirt to wear. I streaked it with water and placed a few heavy notebooks on top of it. After my shower, the shirt almost looked like it had been ironed.

All day long, at school, I tried to determine how angry Craig might be, but since we never talked in public anyway, I couldn't tell. Finally the last bell rang.

ON MY WAY to her house, I spotted Miss Cogshell clambering up the post office steps, so I went to the pier instead. Craig sat at the end in our usual spot.

"Are you waiting for Miss Cogshell to get back?" I asked.

"Yep," he said without turning around.

"You know," I said, "about yesterday . . . "

Waves from the wake of a passing speedboat slapped against the supports below us. I hollered over the noise. "I was only trying to say that how you see yourself isn't how other people see you."

"Really, and how would you know?" His voice had an edge to it.

The words jammed in my throat. There was so much I wanted to tell Craig, but I didn't know how—thoughts were buzzing around in my head like bees in a beehive.

I forced myself to plop down beside him. He didn't know he was the best friend I'd ever had, that he was funny and clever and that every day he grew more special to me. My face got hot just picturing myself trying to express such sappy stuff.

"Sometimes I should mind my own beeswax," I said. "And I'm sorry."

I closed my eyes and felt Craig watching me, a red-faced idiot. He shifted his weight, and his arm brushed mine as he got comfortable. We sat there like two lumps, not speaking for the longest time. The clouds shifted and changed the reflected patterns in the water. I looked over at Miss Cogshell's house and saw the kitchen light was now on.

"When I was a little kid," said Craig, "I used to sit on this dock and think the goofiest things. Like maybe…" he stopped. "Like maybe my dad didn't just take off, maybe he was sitting right here one day and a giant wave came and swallowed him up."

"I used to see you down here a lot. I never guessed you'd be thinking about that kind of stuff."

"Stupid, huh?"

I suddenly felt sad. "No."

Craig gave me a sideways glance and then put an exaggerated pout on his face. I grinned in spite of myself.

Then Craig, who could never stay still for long, jumped up. "Why did the elephant sit on the marshmallow?"

I knew the answer, but shrugged my shoulders.

"So he wouldn't fall in the hot chocolate!"

I laughed more than the joke warranted, just for the fun of it.

"I think of odd things, too," I said as I stood up and brushed off the seat of my jeans.

"Yeh? Like what?"

I shook my head.

"Come on. I told you my weirdo stuff."

"Well, like maybe our whole world is only a speck. In a bigger world."

"Huh?"

"Forget it. I'm just strange."

Craig thought it over a minute. "You mean like the earth could be a dot in an enormous parking lot?"

"Yes! Exactly. You get it."

"But what if a giant steps on us?"

"We'll just have to take our chances."

"Oooh, watch out!" Craig yanked me by the arm to the other side of the pier.

"What?" I shouted, as my head spun in every direction in search of the problem.

"Come here," said Craig, steering me with my elbow. "See that little snail shell? No, not that one. The miniscule one next to it."

I peered down at the shell.

"There's a whole civilization living in there and a giant shrimp almost wiped them out with one lime-green sneaker."

"You're crazy," I said, laughing.

We strolled out to the road.

I was hoping he had forgotten about his progress report, when he mumbled, "My old lady's gonna kill me."

"No she won't." I was still smiling. It felt great to be goofing around with Craig again. "Just explain it to her and tell her you'll try harder next time. And you do still have a few weeks to raise those grades."

"Marston says if my grades don't go up, I'll have to repeat the year."

"Oh." I finally realized how much was at stake. "Well, I'll help you study, and I'm sure Miss Cogshell will too."

"She has been. If it wasn't for Miss C., I probably would've had five Fs."

Craig must have spent more time at Miss Cogshell's than I realized. I glanced out towards the field and whispered, "That was great on the bus yesterday."

"What?" Craig asked, bending closer to hear.

I peeked up at him. "When you yelled 'shut up.'"

"Blowing up is great?" Craig looked genuinely surprised.

"You stood up for Miss Cogshell. I was too chicken."

"Just letting off steam. Didn't take any guts. My old lady says one of these days my temper's gonna get me in real trouble."

We made our way to Miss Cogshell's and hung out with Pup for the rest of the afternoon.

11

MY VISITS TO Miss Cogshell's fell into a happy routine. When I stopped by one day, hoping to borrow a book, she was on a small stool, hunting through her spice cupboard. Her hair brushed the ceiling. As she reached deep into the cabinet, I watched, worried she'd come crashing down. Her flowered housecoat rose, and exposed the rolled tops of her stockings. Through the nylons, dark veins ran up and down her massive calves.

"I was sure I had another tin of ginger," she said. "What a chowduhhead I am. I've already mixed the first ingredients and now I'm out of ginger."

"I'll run down to Al's and get it," I offered.

"Oh, you don't have to do that." Miss Cogshell climbed off the tiny stool, using the counters for support, took a few deep breaths and turned towards me. A faded Maine lobster was stamped across the front of her muslin apron.

"But I want to," I said. "I love ginger cookies."

Miss Cogshell smiled as she reached for a small china teapot. From inside, she produced a tightly folded dollar bill which she opened and pressed flat into my hand. She held it for a moment between her warm, fleshy palms. "Well, in that case, off you go."

Before I finished humming two verses of "The Night the Lights Went Out in Georgia," I was at Al's General Store. I opened the door slowly, the bell keeping still, and went in unnoticed to search the crowded shelves for ginger.

A minute later the bell over the door jingled as someone else entered the store. He struck up a conversation with Al, who must have been behind the counter. I recognized Howard the harbormaster's deep voice ordering a coffee. The squeak of the spinning barstool told me he planned to sit for a while.

Just as I spotted the ginger I heard Al's voice ask, "Any big goings on lately?"

I froze in my tracks when I heard the deep voice answer. "Not much. Although, apparently Ed Johnson thought he saw a couple of kids with a seal up the road apiece, a few weeks back. But you never can tell with his memory. Could've been a cat. I'm keeping my eyes and ears open."

"Ayuh," replied Al. "Poor Ed's always got some tall tale or other. Remember that time he thought my house was on fire when I was burning brush?" Al let out a hearty laugh.

They continued to discuss Mr. Johnson while I crouched two aisles back. I clutched the tin of ginger and tried not to sneeze. Finally the seat creaked and Howard said good-bye to Al. I counted to ten, and then came around the corner real casual. Just as I got to the cash register, the bell over the door jangled again. Two girls from my class came in—one of them being Ed Johnson's daughter, Pamela. The girls didn't see me at first; they were too busy checking out their reflections in the shiny countertop, while Al was in the backroom.

"So Claire, who are you asking?" Pamela was saying.

"Probably Tommy since you want *you know who*," said Claire.

"Remember I told you my dad thought he saw him with some girl the other night," Pamela continued in a sing-songy voice. "Well, my unhelpful father says he can't remember what she looked like, or how late it was; just that they were pulling a seal in a wagon. Can you imagine?" She shook her hair back and then spotted me trying to blend in with the pickle barrel.

"Shrimp, what a surprise! Who are *you* taking to the Twist Twirl?" she asked, all wide-eyed. I just looked at her with no clue as to what she was talking about. The two girls towered above me, their hairspray stinking up the whole store. A limp strand fell across my eye and I wished I'd washed my hair that morning.

"I guess they don't let little kids in." Claire shrugged her shoulders. They both laughed and moved past me down the aisles, stumbling along on their platform shoes. One of them said in a loud whisper, "Why doesn't she ever talk?" A softer whisper was followed by more giggling.

I stared hard at the penny candy until Al returned to ring up my order. Soon I was running back to Miss Cogshell's, back to the smells and sounds of her cozy home.

"Why Amy, you're all out of breath," she said, as I handed her the ginger and a few coins. "Did you have trouble finding it?"

"The harbormaster was there," I said.

"He's an interesting man."

"He heard there might be a captive seal around here."

"Oh, dear," said Miss Cogshell, as she peeled the lid off the top of the ginger. She sprinkled some in without measuring, while I left to go visit Pup.

Pup blinked his round eyes when he saw me, and then gave a great yawn. Sprawled out in a relaxed blubbery heap on the bathroom floor, Pup appeared not to have a care in the world. He stretched, then covered one eye with his fore flipper like he was playing peek-a-boo.

"Don't worry, Pup, nobody will find you here," I whispered into his sleek little head. He sniffed and nuzzled my hair and I could tell he knew me as a friend. I took a fish from the cooler and was glad to see him swallow it right down. By the time I went back to the kitchen, Miss Cogshell was already pulling the baked cookies out of the oven.

"No homework tonight. I sure wish I had a good mystery to read," I hinted as I nibbled a warm cookie.

"Help yourself." She nodded towards the parlor. I went in and studied the titles. Miss Cogshell came in a moment later and we talked about a few of her favorite stories.

Just as I selected a book, loud crashing noises interrupted us. We looked at each other, puzzled, and then I moved fast down the hall. My words froze when I reached the kitchen.

"Oh, no," said Miss Cogshell. I squeezed to one side so she could fit through the entranceway. Cookies were everywhere, mostly on the floor. One cooling rack still teetered half on the table and half off. I glanced at Miss Cogshell and she didn't look pleased. At the same time, we both said, "Pup?"—mine a troubled whisper.

"I'm sure he didn't mean it." I tried not to panic. "I'll clean up." I tossed my book onto the counter, dropped to my knees and began gathering up cookie pieces while she and Clyde stomped down the hallway towards the bathroom.

"Where is that rascal?" she said a minute later.

I heard a little sniff. I spun around and peered beneath the tablecloth. Pup was under the kitchen table, way back against the wall. His nose lay flat on the floor and he closed his big eyes when he saw me. I could hear Miss Cogshell returning.

"I can't find him," she said.

"Are you very angry with him?" I asked.

"Oh, he doesn't know better. I just want to make sure he's not sick from too many sweets."

"I'll get him." I crawled under the table to drag him out.

"Stop acting innocent, Pup," I tried to say with sternness while he playfully nipped my elbow. Miss Cogshell counted cookies and decided he'd probably only tasted one or two. We swept all the crumbs out the back door and made an attempt at scolding Pup, just so he'd remember to keep his nose out of the goodies next time.

Soon I was walking home, tripping over tree roots while absorbed in my book. By bedtime I had finished reading *The Body in the Library*.

AT SCHOOL, THE next day, I passed by a poster and remembered how Pamela had mentioned the Twist Twirl. I had never bothered to read event notices before, but figured I'd do so now. Apparently the Twist Twirl was a school dance to be held in a few weeks.

For this one event the girls got to ask the boys to go with them. Kind of like a Sadie Hawkins Day.

I knew right off who Pamela would want to go with, and then, I don't know what came over me, but I started having this fantasy of *me* walking in with Craig, and Pamela falling off her platform shoes, flat on her face. It wasn't that I just wanted to shock everyone—I really wanted to be at the dance with Craig. We got along so well. He was always laughing and joking with me, so he must like me. As the day wore on, the more excited I got. I would beat Pamela to the punch.

I had never cared before how long Nancy spent blabbing on the phone. However, the one time I wanted to make a call she must have been on for two hours, catching up with all the kids she had just spent the whole day with. After supper I got my chance. Dad was working on bills in his office and Mom took Nancy out to get her hair trimmed. I must have stood by the telephone for ten minutes before I got up the nerve to dial the number I had spent all day memorizing. It rang four times, each time making my heart pound louder. On the fifth ring Craig's mother answered.

"What do you want?" she drawled into the mouthpiece. Her words were slurred and she sounded half-asleep. I panicked and hung up the phone with shaking hands.

"I'll ask him tomorrow," I decided.

~ ~ ~

FRIDAY MORNING, CRAIG stood by himself fiddling around with his locker combination. I watched for a minute from down the hall, and practiced the words I would use to ask him to the dance. As I started over to him, I heard stomping and giggling coming from around the corner.

Great. Pamela and Claire. It was like I was a magnet, always pulling those two closer to wherever I happened to be. Pamela practically fell into Craig as though the corridor was just too narrow for her to get past him. He grinned, the same grin as always. Then Claire made some comment and Craig burst out laughing. I knew they didn't even know I was there, but they might as well have been laughing at me.

I stuck my head back into my locker and pretended to search for something. In my mind I could hear Nancy saying, "Oh, Amy, you're so immature!" My eyes stung. All this time I thought Craig and I had a special friendship; now I finally understood that he just acted that way with everyone. My hands started shaking again when I realized how close I had come to making a fool of myself.

I peeked over my shoulder. Craig took off in the other direction, while the two girls headed my way. Pamela came to a halt in front of me. She squinted her eyes and scrunched up her face. "I know what you're up to," she said, wagging a long polished nail at me before they continued down the hall.

Oh, my gosh. Could she really? I hadn't breathed a word about the dance. There's no way she could find out. Was she just bluffing? Or, worse, was she talking about Pup?

12

ON SATURDAY, I woke to the rattle of wind-driven sleet against the windowpanes. All morning, the rain poured down. I tried to concentrate on a cross-stitch kit, except my eyes kept traveling to the windows, my mind elsewhere. There weren't many more days to be with Pup, especially if Pamela knew about him. Finally I'd had enough. I ran upstairs for the Agatha Christie book, threw on my slicker, and headed for the door.

"Where in the world are you going?" asked Nancy, who looked as bored as me.

"Just out." I stuffed the book under the front of my slicker.

"But, Amy." My mother looked up from her magazine. "It's pouring cats and dogs out there. You'll be soaked through in no time."

"Well, I've just got to run quick down towards the pier. Then I'll be dry."

"To the pier? I don't understand. How will you be dry at the pier?"

I glanced at Nancy and then answered my mother. "Because I'll be in a house down near there."

Nancy laughed. "Yeah, right. The only one who lives down there is Old Coot. She's the one who used to pass out banned books to kids."

My eyebrows went skyward as I pushed Agatha Christie further under my slicker. Nancy puffed herself up and waddled around looking as big and ugly as she could.

"Stop that, Nancy." Mom proceeded to lecture Nancy about name-calling. I could feel the anger rising in me as I took the opportunity to slip out the door. Once again, Nancy had got me furious. There would probably be a lot of explaining to do when I got home; for now though, I just had to get to Pup.

I raced down the hill. I could barely see with the rain slanting into my face. The wind howled and I could hear the surf crash against the shoreline and the grating of haunted lobster boats as they tugged at their moorings.

By the time I reached Miss Cogshell's, I was shivering. She answered my knock as I scraped the mud from my boots. A waft of warm cinnamony smells crept out. Miss Cogshell didn't look at all surprised to see me—almost as though she'd been waiting for me to show up.

I went in and exchanged looks with Craig. He sat at the kitchen table with his math book and papers spread out in front of him.

"Just catching up on some homework," he mumbled.

"We didn't have any," I said, before I caught Miss Cogshell's look.

"I still haven't finished last week's," Craig said. "Not all of us are straight A students. Besides, my house isn't exactly set up for studying." He gave an awkward laugh as he stood and stretched his legs.

Rather than argue about my occasional B, I grinned and pulled out the book. "This was a great mystery, Miss Cogshell."

She nodded. "One of my favorites, too."

I returned the book to its place on the shelf and went in to visit Pup. As I patted Pup, I strained to hear the voices in the kitchen.

"Try this one again," instructed Miss Cogshell. "I know you can do it."

The low mumbling that followed must have been Craig's response. I surely hoped this tutoring would get him into the next grade.

Pup got restless and belly-bounced down the hallway. He turned in at the parlor. I followed, calling out to him. Soon Craig and Miss Cogshell joined us, and we all watched Pup explore and sniff every nook and cranny.

"Your house is always so quiet. Don't you have any TV, Miss C.?" asked Craig, looking around in disbelief. "How can you watch *Hawaii Five-0*?"

"Actually, I do own one. It's right under here." Miss Cogshell pinched up a large doily that had been covering a small television. "Just wait 'til I show you what my friend from Texas sent me." She carefully unrolled a clingy, plastic sheet and stuck it over the screen. Then she turned on the TV. She moved her massive body to one side so we could see. The once black and white pictures now had tints of color filling in all the light areas. Miss Cogshell watched a moment, then glanced over at us.

"That's super," I said.

"*Su*-per," agreed Craig, laughing. "I think I'll stick with Zenith."

"Well, I'm sure this doesn't compete with the new color televisions. Suits me fine just the same."

Miss Cogshell was rolling up the magic color screen when there was a thud and a high pitched squeal from somewhere outside, behind the house.

I spun around. Pup must be in the kitchen! I rushed in, grabbed him in a big hug, and slid him under the table, with me right behind. I had to hide him from whoever was out there. Thank goodness the inside door was closed shut against the last of the rain.

"Aw, geez," said Craig, a couple of seconds after he reached the kitchen.

"She probably slipped and bumped up against the house," said Miss Cogshell when she joined him. "Do you *know* that young lady peeking in the window, Craig?"

Craig must have nodded because Miss Cogshell opened the door. I couldn't believe it when I heard Pamela's voice and recognized the shiny red tips of her mud-splashed boots as she stepped inside.

"My goodness, you'll get drenched," said Miss Cogshell.

I listened to the squeaking of Pamela's matching, hooded slicker and could just imagine her straining her neck to peer past Miss Cogshell in search of Craig.

"Oh hi, Craig," Pamela said. "I thought I saw your bike down here a lot. I just wanted to ask you something, um . . . about homework, in private."

"I was leaving anyway." Craig yanked his jacket off the kitchen chair, inches from my hiding place.

"That was a close call," said Miss Cogshell after the door closed behind them.

I peered out the window and wondered which of a long list of possibilities, each more horrible than the last, Pamela had come to see Craig about.

THAT NIGHT, AFTER I was in bed, the storm still raged outside, sending shadows around the room. My mother gave a soft knock on my bedroom door. I shoved my diary under my pillow, flicked off my flashlight and said, "Yeah?"

"I just wanted to talk a bit," she said, as she squeezed in between the pillows of my window seat. She probably wished she could clear them out, but we had decided long ago that my space was off limits.

"You've always been a good girl and I don't want you to think I'm accusing you of anything. It's just that, well, you're a teenager now, and I'd like to know where you go every day."

She caught me at a relaxed moment, so rather than fight it, I decided to talk to her. "You wouldn't believe me if I told you," I said, smiling into the darkness.

"Try me."

"I go to Miss Cogshell's house."

"For?"

"To visit with her and," I took a deep breath, "a pet of hers."

"Well, that certainly sounds admirable. Your grandmother used to speak quite highly of Sylvia."

"What did Nancy mean about banned books?" I said, knowing something, but wanting to know more.

"Oh, that," Mom said with a sigh. "I guess years ago a group of parents tried to get her fired from her teaching job because she was recommending books they thought inappropriate. Even literature like *Romeo and Juliet*. That sort of thing. Those former students grew up still carrying their parents' anger and passed it down to their own kids."

"Yeah," I said, "probably they started calling her Old Coot, and everyone else just went along with it because she's so different looking."

My mother murmured in agreement. Her satin robe glistened in the dim light that shone in from the hallway. "Sweetie, there's one other thing. Nancy thought she saw you with a boy the other day after school."

Oh, brother. She and Nancy must have discussed me after I left in a huff that morning. "Is that against the law?" I pulled the covers up closer to my chin.

"No, it's just not like you."

"Well, that must have been my friend Craig Miller." I tried not to blush. "He's a friend of Miss Cogshell's, too."

"Craig Miller?" I couldn't see my mother's face in the shadows, which was probably just as well. "That cute little towhead who sat in front of you in first grade? Well, I guess Nancy would be impressed. Seems I heard something about the Millers lately." She thought a minute. "Well, I guess it was probably just gossip. Anyway, so Craig is a teenager now, too."

"You make it sound like being a teenager is a disease."

"Of course not. It's just a difficult time for some." She adjusted the pillows and I could tell she wanted to ask something more. Finally she blurted out, "Is Craig a nice boy?"

"Yes," I said fast. "And Mom, don't tell Nancy. I don't need the whole Port knowing who I'm friends with."

"My baby's growing up." Mom sighed as she stood and smoothed the wrinkles from her housecoat. "Did I ever tell you how Dad and I met?"

"Only a thousand times, but go ahead."

"I couldn't skate for beans. After I crashed into your father, he pulled me around that pond all night, and from then on, we were a couple."

I tried to picture Mom and Dad years ago, young and in love. Now, Mom was always preparing for some party for other people while Dad spent hours in his office. Sometimes he was in there for so long I forgot he was even home. I guess that's why I became such a good reader. I just didn't click with the rest of my family. Nancy's the one Mom should be discussing boys with.

"Mom, Craig and I are just friends. Besides, who wants a stupid ol' boyfriend?"

My mother watched me for a moment, as though seeing right through my words. Then she kissed me goodnight on the forehead. The tapping of the rain against my window lulled me to sleep.

13

WHILE DIGGING IN my closet Sunday morning, I found an old plastic ball. I started to toss it aside until I realized it might be fun for Pup. I washed the ball, and then polished it with my sweater all the way to Miss Cogshell's.

She had just returned from coffee hour at the church and was busy arranging her letter writing supplies. Floral stationery, stickers, stamps, envelopes and her special calligraphy pen were all lined up on the blue-checked cloth.

Not wanting to rush past her each day in my eagerness to see Pup, I slipped into a chair and glanced at the plant cups on her windowsill. "Looks like your lupines are getting bigger."

"Oh, yes, they're coming along." She checked the tip of her pen.

"Who are all these people you write to?" I asked.

"Well, some are from an international pen pal club, and the one from England—she is my old friend from college. Margie, the one who started my collection when she sent me the little penguin."

"You went to college?"

"Yes, I was a school teacher up until 1956."

"Before I was even born," I said, just so she'd know I didn't care what kind of stuff her students had read. "You must have a zillion books."

Miss Cogshell chuckled. "I guess I do have a few."

"So that's how you knew my grandmother, through teaching?"

"Yes, we were both teachers. What a funny pair we made. Me so tall and her so short."

Of course. I'd forgotten. My grandmother was short like me. Since I was just a little kid when she died I had always thought my grandmother was tall like any other adult. But now I remembered from old family pictures how tiny she had stood in front of my tall parents. My mind raced back to the present. "So that's why you're helping Craig."

"I do enjoy teaching. However, I also want to help that poor, lost boy."

"Poor, lost boy?" I looked at Miss Cogshell and decided to set her straight. "Craig's really loud and popular at school."

Miss Cogshell smoothed out a fresh sheet of stationery. "Sometimes people would rather laugh than cry." She dipped her pen into a tiny bottle of ink. "Anyway, I will do what I can for him."

I watched her produce a perfect line of swirly letters, while I tried to make sense of her words. Could a silent shrimp like me, really be happier than a loud happy-go-lucky kid like Craig?

"I might like to be a teacher," I said, surprising myself. "But I don't want to go away to college. I want to stay right here in the Port forever." I flung my arms out to encompass my whole world.

Miss Cogshell looked up from her letter and smiled. "I bet you'll change your mind about college when you are older, Amy. You're a clever girl."

A shuffling noise made us look toward the hallway. Pup was on his way, inching along like a giant caterpillar. I jumped up from my seat to see him better. His floppy little crawl made me laugh. "You're up and about again!"

"Yes, he likes to stretch once in a while." Miss Cogshell turned back to her work.

"I have a surprise for you, Pup." I pulled the small plastic ball from my pocket and kneeling down, spun it slowly towards him. With his nose he pushed it back to me. I rolled it again and he returned it once more. Pup looked like a flabby rubber ball himself, dribbling along after the little plastic one.

Back and forth we played. Then I pushed the ball too hard. It spun past Pup, zigzagged down the hall, bounced off the baseboard and into the parlor. Pup went after it and I followed. His snout went under Miss

Cogshell's big chair while the rest of him flipped up from behind. He couldn't reach it and looked back at me.

"I'll get it, Pup," I said. I sprawled out on the braided rug, wiggled up close to the chair and stretched my arm as far as I could reach. Just as my fingertips brushed the ball, Pup shoved me over and stuck his nose in again. We couldn't both fit, so we kept pushing each other aside. Pup snorted and I pleaded. "I can get it, Pup. Just get out of my way!"

Finally I got hold of the ball and tossed it to Pup. What did he do? He pushed it back under the chair, further than before. "You silly seal," I said, laughing. I knew Pup was happy even though those big tears were just streaming down his face. I hugged him and inhaled his warm fishy smell. I patted his slick little head and whispered, "You're a good friend." I thought about how lonely I had been just a month or so ago and added, "You and Craig and Miss Cogshell." Pup started snoozing right there in my arms. I watched him sleep for a while, and then I gently moved him aside. I tiptoed down the hall and back into the kitchen to find Miss Cogshell still seated at the table.

Her finished letter, curling up as it dried, was tossed to one side. There was a tender look in her eyes as she studied her hands. On her left plump pinky was a silver band I had never seen before.

I cleared my throat. She glanced up, found me watching her, then struggled to get the band from her finger. Pink color rose in her cheeks from the exertion. "It must have shrunk." Miss Cogshell chuckled as the ring popped off. She dropped it into a small gray box on the table.

"Is that a new ring?" I asked.

"Not unless you call fifty-five years old, new." She pulled her heavy frame out of the chair.

"I've never seen you wear a ring before."

"That's because I haven't worn it in over fifty years."

I knew I should stop questioning her, but I wanted to understand that look I had seen on her face. She lumbered down the hall to her bedroom.

I inspected the little gray box. Although worn now, I could tell it once had a fuzzy velveteen texture. Its lid made a satisfying click. I snapped it open and shut several times. A small, yellowed paper fit snugly inside the cover. A faded heart was drawn on it with the words 'To Sylvia' written inside the heart. I tried to picture Miss Cogshell as a young Sylvia. It was difficult.

I was completely engrossed in snooping when I sensed I wasn't alone. I looked up to find her in the doorway. She held a picture frame.

"Sorry," I said. "I'm just too curious."

"I was cleaning out a drawer this morning and happened to find the ring."

"Was it a gift?"

"Stanley Whitmore gave the ring to me when we became engaged."

"Engaged?" I blurted out.

"For one year we were engaged while Stanley fought in the war."

"I didn't know you'd been married," I said with a giggle.

"We planned . . . " Miss Cogshell stopped, then said briskly, "We planned to get married, only he did not make it back."

Heat swirled through my temples and knocked the proper response right out of my brain. For the life of me I couldn't speak.

"I know it is hard to imagine me with a sweetheart, Amy, but . . . "

"No," I protested with vigorous head shaking.

She flipped over the little frame she had brought in from the other room and placed it in front of me. "Stanley was a lobsterman who just couldn't get enough of my raspberry pies," she said with fondness.

I studied the smiling couple. Could that really be Miss Cogshell and her *boyfriend*? The photo showed a husky girl with good posture and a long, pale braid draped over one shoulder. She carried what appeared to be a picnic basket. The lanky man beside her was a couple of inches shorter. He had a friendly, open face and one of his arms curled around the girl's waist. An old Model T was parked behind them.

"I want you to know that Stanley tried to come home to me, but God had other plans for him. Now he is in the little graveyard behind my church." Miss Cogshell reached for the ring box and turned it over several times in her hands. "The saddest part was that he was shot down just days before the war ended."

"I'm so sorry," I stammered, as my eyes filled with tears. I visualized the sturdy young girl receiving such dreadful news while everybody else cheered the end of World War I.

"It is okay now. Past is past." She let out a long sigh. She picked up the box and picture, dropped them into her housecoat pocket, and then busied herself packing up writing supplies. "Let's make cookies."

EVERY AFTERNOON THAT week I visited Miss Cogshell and Pup for a couple of hours. It made me wonder what on earth I used to do after school. Craig was there most days, the best days. We would walk over to the pier on our way home and more often than not have one of our deep conversations. Although he always joked around with everyone at school, I had a feeling Craig saved the serious stuff for me. He knew his secrets were safe, since I didn't say boo to anyone else.

Sometimes I'd see Pamela and Claire snooping around. I'd hide behind the woodshed until the coast was clear. I discovered that it took exactly five minutes for them to stroll from the end of the pier to the post office. When they got past Miss Cogshell's yard, I'd make a run for the back door.

Once, Craig got caught turning into the walkway on his bike. I watched them through the ivy that hung in the kitchen window. They laughed and talked about who knows what. I stopped spying after Pamela redid her ponytail for the third time. Later, Craig mentioned that Pamela had said, "Oh, what a coincidence!" I didn't bother to tell him I had counted them going past the house nine times that morning, because then he might have figured out that I'd been watching for him, too.

I never did get up the nerve to invite him to the dance and eventually decided he probably wasn't into that sort of thing anyway. I mean, it would be hard to picture him standing at a dance in that droopy, old army jacket. I convinced myself that I wasn't into dances either. They were more of a Nancy kind of event.

Miss Cogshell was always baking cookies and telling us stories about the old times while we watched Pup's funny antics. I had never been allowed a pet in our polished showplace of a home, and Craig's mother had allergies. *Supposedly*, he said. So we enjoyed and loved our fast-growing Pup like he was our very own. None of us mentioned that he was a temporary pet, though I knew we all were aware of the days swiftly passing.

14

CRAIG WASN'T IN school one Friday, and I had a dentist appointment right after. But first thing Saturday, I threw on an old sweatshirt and a pair of dungarees and went to Miss Cogshell's. She was in her backyard hanging laundry on the clothesline. Bleach-scented sheets puffed up slowly, bright against the green pines. Sunlight defined the many fine lines on her face. Removing a clothespin from her mouth, she said, "Go on in, I'll be another minute."

I could hear Pup splashing and followed the noise into the bathroom. Craig was sitting on the floor next to the tub. At first I thought it was the shower curtain that made a shadow on his face, but then I realized he had a long, thin bruise on his cheek. I was about to ask what happened, when the back door slammed. Wordlessly, I knelt beside Craig.

Soon Miss Cogshell filled the hallway, and the three of us watched Pup in silence. I listened to Miss Cogshell's cuckoo clock ticking from the parlor. I shifted my position and peeked at my friends. A feeling that something else wasn't right began to creep over me. When Craig spoke, I knew what it was.

"Me and Miss C. were talking and we think since the weather's supposed to be nice and all, we should let Pup go—tomorrow."

"It will be quiet on a Sunday morning," added Miss Cogshell.

"Besides," said Craig, "it's getting harder to keep Pup secret. Some kids at school asked about him."

"Gee, I wonder why?" I said in my best snotty voice. "Nosy, big-mouth Pamela, that's why," I spit out. I glanced up quick at Miss Cogshell, and her raised eyebrows made me feel ashamed. I knew I wasn't really angry with Pamela; I was angry at losing Pup.

My mind raced. Tomorrow! No more Pup? It was hard to swallow. "Do you think he'll be okay in the ocean?" I asked. Craig and I exchanged looks, but there didn't seem to be any answers.

"Let me tell you a true story about the ocean." Miss Cogshell motioned for us to follow her into the parlor.

That parlor—such a cozy place, with dark flowery wallpaper and the constant ticking of the cuckoo clock. Three of the walls had books right up to the ceiling. The other had the fireplace and that silly little doily-covered TV. A small pillow stuffed with pine needles let off a strong woodsy scent. There was something about Miss Cogshell's house that made it different from any other. Each room was filled with things she loved. I glanced at Craig and realized we became part of her rooms, too. I wondered if he had ever noticed her bread dough smell. We stretched out on the braided rug while Miss Cogshell settled into her big chair. She leaned Clyde against the arm, pushed her glasses up, and began.

"I will never forget the time God fed the town. Must have been around 1930. The depression had hit and folks were pretty hungry. I was down at the little beach over in Thomaston. I used to go there often. The rush of waves and vastness of the sea always made my own small troubles seem insignificant." She paused a minute while the cuckoo did its thing. "Anyway, that day the waves were stupendous. They'd dash up, slap the shore, then fall back, each time leaving more hake flipping and flopping all over the beach. People started going crazy catching those fish. I hiked up the bottom edges of my long dress and stuffed a bunch of fish in the tote it made. I felt like the Pied Piper delivering hake all over the Port.

"Every day us Mainers came for food until finally we could take no more. People came from as far as Rockland to load up big barrels with fish. A few weeks later the season ended as suddenly as it had begun. I have never again heard of anything like it, in all these years."

"Wow," I murmured, still caught up in the story.

"Is that for real?" asked Craig.

"The ocean is a powerful friend," Miss Cogshell said. "It takes from us, but gives back so much more. Pup will be in good hands."

CRAIG AND I hung around later than usual that day. He did some chores for Miss Cogshell while I tried to memorize everything about Pup, right down to the little heart-shaped spot above his eye. I let him know how much I cared, by patting and playing with him. When pink reflections came in through the newly replaced screen door and the clock gave an extra cuckoo, we knew we'd stayed long enough.

Miss Cogshell slid a blue mothball-scented cardigan sweater over her plump shoulders and stepped outside with us to admire the sky. "Should be a perfect day to let Pup go."

"How come?" Craig peered out beneath his bangs to look up.

"Oh, I know," I said, suddenly remembering the old local saying. "Red in the morning, sailors take warning. Red sky at night, sailors delight."

Craig rolled his eyes. "How could I forget."

"Still a little chilly at night." Miss Cogshell started to head back inside. Then she stopped at the big bush beside the door and gently lifted the buds between her fingers. "Wait 'til you see these lilacs. I look forward to them every year. Just a few more weeks and their color and scent will fill the yard with beauty." She shivered and pulled her sweater tighter around her. "Brrrr—you two better be on your way."

"See ya tomorrow," said Craig taking off on his bike.

Miss Cogshell and I watched him go, then I looked around the yard and back at the house, moving closer to it. "You know," I started to say, unsure what was to follow, "There's something about your house."

Miss Cogshell nodded with a wistful smile on her face.

I searched for a word to describe the way I felt. "Something special, I guess."

"Oh, Amy, I am so glad you feel it, too. I'm sure it is not everyone's cup of tea. Years ago I made up a will and left this house to Port Wells. What a comfort to know it will always be here by the pier, appreciated by people like you."

"Don't say that," I blurted out. "I mean . . . " I looked down at my sneakers. "You're not going anywhere."

Miss Cogshell patted my shoulder and then chuckled.

Confused, I glanced up at her jolly expression.

"I'm just remembering one of my father's sayings. Every time my mother worried about some health issue, he'd say, 'None of us is getting out of here alive!'"

"But, death is so scary."

"Not really. No more frightening than birth. Who knows, it could be as beautiful as life itself. Experience all your dreams and you'll have no regrets."

As she pulled me close with her big arms I couldn't for the life of me imagine her not always being there.

ON MY WAY home, the air smelled strongly of wood smoke. Soft yellow lamplight glowed in a few of the houses. People under the lights prepared for the evening; unaware I was moving past in the darkness.

Later, climbing the stairs to my room, I could hear noises coming through Nancy's open door. I paused in the shadowed hallway to peek in. She and Mom sorted through a heap of clothes on the bed. You'd think it was her wedding day the way they were going on and on about the different outfits.

"Okay, then," said Mom. "How about this cute little pantsuit?"

"I wore that to the last party," wailed Nancy. "Besides, I don't want to look cute. There'll be juniors and even seniors there." She held up a black mini skirt. "Maybe this."

Mom sighed. "Only if you wear solid-colored tights and sensible shoes. You're such a pretty girl . . . "

Feeling more alone than a ship lost at sea, I tiptoed down the hallway to my own room while Nancy learned about the dangers of dressing cheap.

I curled up on my window seat in my old sweatshirt and stared out into the dark woods, already missing Pup.

15

I WOKE UP way earlier than I needed to that Sunday and found I had no appetite for breakfast. I spent as long as Nancy would to select an outfit: fluorescent yellow sweatshirt with an orange collar sticking out and my plaid bellbottoms, and then I even took a few minutes to comb my freshly shampooed hair. I counted the steps to the little gray house by the pier, and kept my eyes off the deep, dark ocean: Pup's future home. Would I ever see him again? I hung around outside until I saw Craig coming fast down the road on his bike.

"How long ya been here?" he hollered.

"Couple minutes." I watched him toss his bike aside. "I don't know if she's up yet."

Craig held his hand up to shade his eyes, "Whoa."

"What?" I said, glancing down.

"You sure do like bright colors."

"I do." I admired my cheerful sleeve. "Although sometimes I wonder if we all see it the same way."

"Here we go again. Why wouldn't we?"

"Nothing. Forget it." I started to move towards Miss Cogshell's door.

"Hey, you can't leave me hanging. Whaddya mean?" Craig blocked my path. "Tell me about colors, Teach."

"Well, maybe what I see as yellow, you see as blue."

"Why? If that's yellow and that's blue and we both agree, then we see it the same."

"But we'll never know if they're really the same. Not unless I crawled into your head and peered out through your eyes and compared it to how I see it."

"No. That's where I draw the line. You're way too squirmy to be crawling around in my head. Hmm, you'd probably fit though."

I gave him a whack and laughed.

Craig took a few sniffs. "Do you smell somethin'?"

My eyes widened. "Hmmm. It's ginger. It's what I smelled the first time I came here."

"It worked out good, Amy," Craig said with a big smile.

I stood as still as the pine trees, letting the sound of Craig saying my name seep through me. The very first time he had ever said it. I managed to blurt out, "What?"

"Coming to her house."

I grinned. "I told you so."

"No, I mean it. Things are gonna be much better now. It's weird how sometimes really bad things like losing Pup can happen at the same time as really good things." Craig faced the sun as he looked at me. His eyes were bright. "My mom's gonna go to a treatment center. Maybe she'll get well this time."

"Get well? What's wrong?"

"Are you serious?" Craig asked with both eyebrows up. "You don't know?"

I tried to put the right expression on my face, but I had no clue as to what he was talking about.

"My old lady's a drunk. I thought the whole Port knew. Once, when Ma came looking for me, Miss C. chewed her out and gave her a book about alcoholism. Mom was furious, but I guess it eventually sank in."

I wanted to say so many things to Craig right then except they got all jumbled in my throat, so I looked stupidly at my feet. By the time I came up with something, my chance was gone. Craig never talked serious for long.

"The smell of ginger also means," Craig paused for effect, "that Miss C.'s up." We raced to the door and gave two quick raps.

"Come in, come in," called out Miss Cogshell, pulling the door open. "I'm just making sure my camera is working. Pup ate four fish this morning, so he's all set."

"Did I really used to lug this lump of lard?" Craig looked at Pup with fondness. "He's put on a lot of weight."

"He's a good little seal," said Miss Cogshell as she placed a large carton nearby.

I couldn't say anything. My teeth started chattering foolishly.

Miss Cogshell propped open the screen door while we carried Pup through in the box. "Watch my lilac bush," she cautioned as we squeezed past. "Now where did Clyde get off to?"

I peered back inside and spotted her cane. "There he is, on the table."

"Okay then, kiddos. I guess we're ready."

A clunk-clunk sound told me the Harbormaster's truck was rounding the bend. I scooched down in front of the box that held Pup, and Craig did the same. Howard slowed down and peered over at us. I gave him a cheery wave. He was probably thinking: *hmm, when did she get so friendly?* But no matter, it worked and he drove on down the road.

Craig and I pulled Pup in the cardboard box, over to the pier. Miss Cogshell came along behind us with her Kodak camera swinging from a strap about her neck. Her breathing seemed labored for such a short walk, and that poor little turtle was doing all it could to hold her up.

It was a bright, clear day and I could see faraway Wàwàckèchi Island easily. Why not rain today?

"Did you ever notice how in the movies it always rains during funerals?" said Craig.

I nodded. How did he know I was just thinking that?

We brought the box right to the little beach where Craig had found Pup many weeks ago. Craig ripped open one side, so Pup would be able to leave on his own. We both reached out for Pup at the same time, needing to keep him with us that extra minute. It was a sloppy hug, the three of us entwined. I could hear the click of Miss Cogshell's camera. Then, as if on cue, we both let go and Pup waddled out of the box. Without hesitation he bellied over to the shoreline.

"Go for a swim, Pup!" said Craig. Pup sniffed the water's edge, then flapped one flipper in.

"That's a good boy," said Miss Cogshell, with a chuckle. "He's testing the temperature."

One of the last slabs of ice rolled in and Pup crawled aboard and floated out on it. Then he turned towards us and cocked his head.

"You're on your own, Pup." Craig's voice cracked on the last words.

Pup slid off the ice and swam in a few circles. He snorted and twitched his whiskers, clumsy until he reached deeper water. Pup dived.

I searched the waves. Was this it? Just dump him in and leave? I bit my lip to keep the tears from spilling out.

"There he is!" shouted Craig. He pointed at the small, shiny head poking up between two buoys.

"Bye, Pup," I managed to call out.

Craig attempted to say goodbye too. His voice sounded like a hiccup. He covered it up by coughing, followed by an energetic wave of his hand.

Pup started to come towards us just under the surface, then breached with a great leap and slapped the water. Under he went again heading out to sea.

"I think he is happier already," said Miss Cogshell. "I'm sure he will meet up with some new friends real soon."

I figured she was just trying to make us feel better.

"He'll be fine," added Craig. He didn't look as sure as he sounded. I began to understand what Miss Cogshell had said about him. He looked like a little lost boy standing there in the big army jacket with his wide blue eyes, the long, thin bruise spotlighted in the sun. Because of it being such an emotional day, I had this silly urge to hug him. I tore my eyes away, and concentrated on a piece of seaweed beneath my sneaker. I pressed hard on the slimy, seaweed bubbles, straining to hear the squishy popping sound.

We watched the empty water for a while longer, and then trudged back to the house in silence. This time Miss Cogshell led the way. She slowly paced herself over the dirt and rocks. I had the feeling we were sad about more than just losing Pup. At one point as we walked, Craig's hand caught mine for the briefest of moments. Then again, maybe his hand just bumped mine by accident.

We ended up in Miss Cogshell's kitchen, although none of us had the appetite to eat ginger cookies. Would there be any reason to ever come again and be in this kitchen, all of us together? I guessed I would come, but what about Craig?

It seemed to take forever for Miss Cogshell's labored breathing to settle down.

"That really wasn't much of a hike." Craig gave a teasing poke in her big, bread dough arm.

"Oh, this is nothing. I'm just an old lady."

"You look a little pale," I said. "Have you had a check-up lately?"

Miss Cogshell chuckled. "I don't need any young whippersnapper to tell me what I already know. Years ago I had a check-up and the doctor said not enough blood gets to my brain, causing these little spells I sometimes get. They wanted to do all these fancy things to fix me up, and now I have probably outlasted them all. I'll leave this good life the way I lived it: fat and happy."

Then it was Miss Cogshell's turn to poke Craig, who seemed to be agreeing with her philosophy. "That doesn't mean you give up your check-ups. The good Lord sent you two to me, to show you what not to do."

After a while there was a knock on the door. Miss Cogshell positioned her plump hands apart on the table, and huffing, hoisted herself up to peek out the window.

"Why, it's that nice harbormaster again," she said.

"Again?" said Craig. We exchanged puzzled looks.

Miss Cogshell opened the door wide. "Come in, Howard."

He removed his hat, nodded at both Craig and I, and then looked back at Miss Cogshell. "I'm sorry to bother you. I've just had another report about there being a seal down this way." Howard was not small, but Miss Cogshell made him look petite. We all stared at him with blank faces.

"Why don't you take a look around to ease your mind," offered Miss Cogshell. "I am very certain there isn't a seal in my house."

Howard seemed embarrassed, but managed to squeeze past us and into the hallway, to poke his head into each room. If it was Pamela who was reporting us, I was sure thankful she hadn't ruined our morning goodbye. I started wondering where I had left Pup's little ball. If only Howard really could find Pup, just so I could see him one more time. But the house was silent—no sniffs, snorts, or belly slapping coming down the hall.

A minute later, Howard came back satisfied that there weren't any illegal animals hidden in the house. "My apologies," he said. "It won't happen again."

"No, I can assure you it will not." A smile tugged on Miss Cogshell's lips. "Take a cookie, Howard."

As soon as Howard's truck pulled out of the yard, we all started laughing. It broke the tension and I was able to eat two ginger cookies after all.

"His face sure gets red," said Craig.

"Oh, we go way back," laughed Miss Cogshell. "Ever since Howie flunked my seventh grade English test, he hasn't been able to look me in the eye."

"Did he really?" said Craig.

"I would have liked to have you for a teacher," I said. Miss Cogshell reached over and patted my hand.

"I'm out of here," announced Craig. "I'll let you two confiscate some verbs together."

"It's *conjugate*, Craig." Miss Cogshell's big shoulders shook with suppressed laughter as we said bye to Craig.

Miss Cogshell watched me peer through the door after him. "You like that boy, don't you?"

I felt myself turn about ten shades of red. "I'm just wondering when those lilacs are going to bloom."

16

DURING THE NEXT week I kept busy. I popped into Miss Cogshell's every other day for quick visits. Sometimes I would borrow a book from her collection.

"Let's plant those lupines," I said one day, glancing at the overflowing cups on her windowsill.

"Today?" she said.

"Sure, why not?"

"Well, yes. Yes, I suppose we could. Just give me a moment to get ready."

I hunted around until I found an old shoebox. Eight little plant cups fit snuggly into the lid, while the leftovers filled the box. "What can we dig with?" I asked.

Miss Cogshell's voice trailed down the hall and I heard the word woodshed.

"Okey-dokey!" I gave the screen door a shove with my knee, carried the boxes of pots out, and placed them along the edge of the back step. Then I hurried over to one of my favorite places. I pushed up the bolt and creaked open the heavy woodshed door. The smell of stale wood shavings filled my nose and I sneezed. As my eyes adjusted to the dim light, I saw tools of all sizes. Stuffed in a web-filled old pot was a small trowel. I poked at it, pulled it out quick and then carried it back between two fingers. Miss Cogshell was just letting the screen door slam behind her.

"Oh, my!" I covered my mouth quick, not meaning to speak aloud.

Like a walking picnic blanket, she wore a massive plaid shirt that must have been a man's size super extra-large. Her big rubber galoshes squeaked as she came down the steps. With Clyde securely under one arm, she paused and adjusted the ribbons of a flower-covered oversized straw hat, under her chins.

"Can't garden without my sun bonnet," she said.

Smiling, I decided to stretch this little project out. It would probably take me all of ten minutes to pop the plants in the ground, which was hardly worth the entertainment of seeing Miss Cogshell in her garden gear. We planted a tidy row of lupines in a dirt strip along the back of the clothesline area.

Miss Cogshell instructed me on how deep and how far apart to plant them. "They'll get good sun here," she said. I doubt she could have bent down far enough, so I was happy I could help her out. Besides, it ended up being a fun way to pass the afternoon.

❧ ❧ ❧

I STAYED DOWN at the pier later than usual that night, just sitting and thinking. After so much excitement over the past few months, life seemed dull. A melon-sliced moon perched high in the sky, its shine catching the crests of never-ending waves.

Finally, I pulled myself up and began the trudge home. With such a narrow moon, it felt like the middle of the night as I crossed the field. The blue glow of televisions shone in several windows out on the road. I scooted across and ducked into the woods.

At first I didn't hear the shuffling noise, my thoughts were so deep. Then I stopped and listened.

Up ahead—great thrashing sounds mixed with the crunching of twigs and pine needles as though under a heavy step. Was Pamela still playing her spying games? I peered up through the trees. Only blackness. Up towards the left was where the moon should be but it was almost as though some giant creature blocked the light. My chest started heaving, and my hands shook.

I tried to scold myself. You're being ridiculous, Amy. Pull yourself together. It's probably just a squirrel in the old elm. I edged over to the nearest tree on my right and slid behind it, willing my breathing to silence. The crashing got louder and closer. I shut my eyes tight. My teeth chattered, so I clamped my hand over my mouth. Sweat dribbled down my back. Thud, thud, as though the very ground shook. Then I heard a snort.

Oh my gosh. Oh my gosh, please don't let this be how I end! I cracked open one eye and watched the massive shape approach. A gross, musky smell filled my nose as the thing ambled by, so close I could have touched it. The short tail swished. It was a moose!

I continued to hug the tree as I tried to make out the giant shape moving down the hill to the road. When I could no longer see it, I counted to ten and then ran as fast as my shaking legs could move me.

I shoved through the front door, slammed it shut behind me and collapsed on the floor of the entranceway.

Nancy paused mid-step on her way upstairs. "Now what?"

"A mooo"—pant pant—"I saw a . . . "

"You saw a moo?" Nancy laughed. "Yes, there are cows out at Drake's farm. What were you doing way out there?"

I shook my head furiously and slowed my breathing. "No. I saw a moose."

"Ah, you finally got your wish! I've seen plenty. No big deal. Really." She gave a slight shake of her curler-covered head and continued to climb the stairs.

I pulled myself together and flew to my diary.

As I was starting to fall asleep, I remembered it was the night of the Twist Twirl. I glanced at the glow-in-the-dark numbers on my clock. 10:30. The dance would be in full swing and almost over. I pictured the music, decorations, and happy kids. I wondered if Craig was home, too. Or was he at the dance—slow dancing with some other girl? My mind spun with what could have been. I found myself acting like Nancy, wishing that he would call me someday. But I was praying for the wrong thing.

REPORT CARD DAY was the day before the last day of school. Our teacher, Mrs. Marston, passed them out in the usual way, alphabetically. I peeked at my good grades and then turned it upside down and waited for Craig to get his. I crossed my fingers that he would at least get promoted.

As Mrs. Marston moved towards him, Craig's leg started bouncing more than usual. He glanced out the window, looking cool as ever, but now I knew better. Knew he was worrying as much as me. Mrs. Marston stopped at his desk and broke into a rare smile. Craig glanced at the report, his eyes wide, then he leaped up onto his desk chair, raised the report high overhead, and shouted.

"Yahoo, I did it!"

Never one for disorder, Mrs. Marston's smile faded faster than the island in fog, but Craig was already jumping down and heading towards me. "Look at that," he said pointing out the C+ in English.

"Nice job," I said, as he moved on towards the open window.

"I did it!" he shouted again to the outside world. Luckily, the dismissal bell rang before Mrs. Marston could send him to the office to spend his last minutes of the school year confessing to the principal. I'm sure she was thrilled Craig was moving on to another teacher.

THAT EVENING, I was washing the dishes after supper when the phone rang. Two long rings and one short—our signal on the party line. Nancy ran to answer since it was always for her. I turned off the water and heard her say, "Amy?" Two seconds later she burst into the kitchen.

"Amy, phone," she announced and then added in an amazed whisper, "It's a boy!" From the look on her face, you'd think I had just won a million dollars. I yanked off my yellow rubber dishwashing gloves, figuring there was some mistake, like a wrong number.

"Hello."

"Amy? Craig. I'm at Miss C's." I felt my face get hot as I glanced up to see Nancy still hanging around the doorway. I waved my hand at her to get lost, so I could concentrate. Nancy rolled her eyes as she backed around the corner, all but one foot anyway.

"She fell," continued Craig.

My mouth opened, yet no words came out, only unwelcome images as I waited for his next words.

"She's okay, but I need help getting her up."

"I'll be right there." I hung up the phone and bolted out the front door, leaving Nancy standing with her mouth hanging open.

"What about the dishes?" she yelled after me. "I'm telling Mum!"

17

MINUTES LATER I pushed through Miss Cogshell's backdoor. She was sprawled the length of the kitchen. Craig, pale beside her.

"She won't let me call an ambulance," he said.

"I'm fine," said Miss Cogshell, panting. "I've gotten these little spells before, just need help getting up."

"But how did you fall?" I asked. A shiver raced through me. My teeth chattered and I grabbed the table edge for support. There was something scary about seeing a grownup so helpless.

"I was reaching for my pen on the floor and the next thing I knew I was down here. If my arm wasn't feeling so useless, I'd probably have popped right up long ago."

Craig and I exchanged glances as I took one side of her and he took the other. We slowly heaved her up onto a chair. Miss Cogshell's cheeks went pale with the exertion and her breathing sped up.

"There . . . the old coot's okay now." She paused for a few breaths. "I don't know what I would do without you two."

I glanced at Craig and wondered how he had happened to be here. His report card was lying on the kitchen table next to a messy pile of S & H green stamps.

"Can I make you some tea, Miss Cogshell?" I asked.

"Oh, I don't want to be a bother. I'll just rest."

"You've done so much for us. I can at least make you tea." I filled the flowered teapot with water. The early evening sun bounced off the curio cabinet and I studied the small animals while the water heated up. So much had happened since I first discovered the porcelain moose.

After placing Miss Cogshell's teacup on the table, I looked over at Craig, who was quiet for once.

"I think she's asleep," he said.

I watched Miss Cogshell for a minute. She seemed comfortable in the high-backed chair. Her breathing was even, and her face with its color returned, seemed almost beautiful in the dim light.

I glanced back at Craig and found him watching her, too. "Thanks for calling me," I said softly. It felt odd to be the smallest kid in my grade lifting the largest woman in the Port.

Craig seemed to read my mind. "You're not exactly Hercules, but who else am I gonna call?" He laughed too loud at his own joke. We glanced at Miss Cogshell again. She slept on, and I was cheered by her recovery.

"I hope my report card wasn't too much of a shock," he added.

I grinned. I drew my fingernail along the blue checks of the tablecloth, feeling shy and wishing Pup was around for us to talk about.

Miss Cogshell began to murmur. Her face went pale as I watched, almost gray now, and her words came out slurred. What a difference from just a few minutes ago. She didn't look like her old self now. I moved over to her.

"Are you okay, Miss Cogshell?"

Her eyes opened and fluttered a bit. It took her a moment to focus on us. "These spells are nothing new… but… if anything should happen," she began.

I got a sick feeling in me waiting for her to finish. Already I was shaking my head, to tell her everything would be all right.

Miss Cogshell continued, "Make sure . . . " she took a few deep breaths, "you develop the pictures." It was hard to make out what she said as she pointed at her camera lying on the table.

"You'll be okay, Miss C.," Craig insisted.

"Let me call your doctor," I urged. She shook her head no. I took Clyde from his resting place by the door and placed him on the table within easy reach. "Or maybe you could stay with a friend?"

I waited for her answer. A plump robin flew past the open kitchen window and landed on the lilac bush. Its sweet fragrance reached me. As if in greeting, the cuckoo clock called out seven times.

Miss Cogshell shook her head again, regaining a little strength, but still speaking slow. "Been in this house eighty years…won't be leaving 'til they have to carry me out. Just need to rest now." She waved her hand and made a feeble attempt at shooing us away.

Craig pocketed his report card and we both squeezed through the door, peering back at her.

"Should we get help anyway?" said Craig.

I nodded. "Let's tell my mom." We broke into a run at the bottom of the hill and arrived at my house, gasping.

"I'll wait here," Craig said as I shoved open the front door. I flew into the house and found my mother dusting in the living room. I blurted out all that had happened since the phone call.

"I don't like the sound of it." My mother put her feather duster aside. "It can't be too healthy to carry all that extra weight around for so many years. I'll call up Mary. She can meet me over there. Mary's had some medical training, and she and Howard go to Miss Cogshell's church. If that doesn't work out, I'll call the doctor myself. Sometimes you have to ignore stubborn people and do what's best for them."

"She'll be okay though, won't she?" I asked, as I watched my mother flip through her phonebook. She gave a helpless shrug and started dialing the phone number.

A few minutes later, the three of us were hurrying towards Miss Cogshell's. I glanced back at our house and saw Nancy's silhouette withdraw from her upstairs window. We stumbled down the hill in silence. Mary's car was already pulling onto the side of the yard when we arrived.

Just before going in, my mother turned to us. "You can go home, kids. I'm sure she'll be fine." We both nodded.

"Well, see you," I said, turning to Craig.

"Yeah, see ya." He continued to stand there.

"Aren't you leaving?" I asked.

Craig shrugged. "Aren't you?"

Neither of us made a move. We stood outside Miss Cogshell's door, about ten feet apart, watching the moon coming up low over the ocean. All was quiet except for the distant creaking of boat lines. Gentle waves slapped the pier posts and the scent of pine filled the air.

I still couldn't get my teeth to stop chattering and the cool evening breezes didn't help. I rubbed my arms, feeling so alone, when suddenly I felt a weight fall across my shoulders. The army jacket. I glanced at Craig, narrower in his tee shirt than I'd seen him in a long time. Shyness overwhelmed me, but Craig didn't seem to have any trouble finding a subject.

"Hey, Shrimp, I didn't see you at the Twist Twirl," he said easily. I started to cringe at the nickname. I looked at Craig and saw no hostility, just friendship. Then I realized what the rest of his words meant. I looked down fast as I felt my stomach sink. I should have known.

"Did you go with Pamela?" I whispered.

"I did. I waited to give her an answer for a couple of weeks. Then I figured since no one else asked me, why not." Craig gave his usual big grin. "Wanna know the truth?" he added. "I'd heard the band did a wicked version of "Layla," so I had to check it out."

I breathed a silent sigh of relief. Was he telling me this for a reason? Or was it just my crazy imagination again? I pictured flashy Pamela and pimply Shrimp standing beside each other. "Was it good?"

"Yeh, they didn't butcher my favorite guitar piece too much."

Miss Cogshell's door opened, and Mom came out.

"You kids should have gone home long ago," she said, as I quickly slipped out of Craig's jacket and tossed it to him. "Miss Cogshell seems fine now. I guess she's had this problem before. She says she's got a few more years in her, and Mary's going to stay with her tonight."

My mother and I said bye to Craig, and he went off in the other direction, while we turned towards our hill.

"So what did you think of her house?" I asked, glad to have shared my special place.

"Didn't really notice too much except that it does need a good cleaning."

"Oh, Mom." I rolled my eyes. "You'll never change."

LATER THAT NIGHT, the wind picked up and the shadow of the old pine tree swaying on my window shade drove me crazy. Maybe tonight would be the night it would come crashing through. And worse, what if Miss Cogshell wasn't back to her cheery self, come morning? I just lost Pup. No way could I lose Miss Cogshell, too. I watched and worried, flipping my pillow over and over in search of a cool place to rest my head.

18

WHEN I PASSED by Miss Cogshell's house the next morning on the school bus, everything seemed as usual. My mother had talked with Mary and apparently all was well.

Before the first bell rang, Craig and I were at our lockers when Pamela and Claire came stumbling along on their platform shoes. I had planned on saying hi to Craig before they came. As I closed my locker I realized how ridiculous I was. Why shouldn't I say hi to my friend, no matter who was around? This was the last day of school; it was now or never. I straightened, turned, and started past them, then forced my head around and said "Hi, Craig."

"Hi, Shrimp," he answered.

Pamela and Claire stared at me. Then Pamela said, "Hi, Shrimp," mocking Craig's words.

I ignored her and focused on my task. "You know, Craig." I paused and took a breath. "I really don't like that name." I almost didn't recognize my strong, clear voice.

Craig lifted one eyebrow. Then he snapped his fingers a few times like he was trying to place me. Finally he pointed and said, "You will be Amy from now on." He smiled that great grin of his, followed by a mock salute in my direction.

What a goof. I had to smile.

As I walked away I heard Pamela and Claire exchange whispers and giggles, but I had a super sure feeling inside me that I would never hear the name Shrimp again.

SO THE DAY had started well, but sometimes things change quicker than a storm at sea. Riding home on the bus that afternoon, an ambulance passed us, lights flashing. It pulled into Miss Cogshell's yard. The bus was silent for once as we watched the ambulance workers rush in.

Craig got off at his usual stop and I saw him sprint down the lane to Miss Cogshell's. I jumped off at the next stop and ran back to stand beside him. I doubted there was anything either of us could do, but I wanted to be there.

Finally her back door swung open. They lugged Miss Cogshell on a stretcher past her beloved lilac bush, finally in full bloom. An oxygen mask hid her face. Her white hair, still so full of life, swung down in long strands on either side of her. A sheet almost covered the mask. What were they thinking?

"Get that off!" I tried to shout, but only air escaped my gasping breath. I wanted to storm over and pull the sheet off, so she could breathe.

Craig must have read my mind. With a firm hold, he grabbed my arm. "I think we lost her," he said.

I shook my head no, back and forth. I felt Craig's grip release as they lifted her into the ambulance. Mary climbed in after them. Through blurry eyes I watched them speed up the road. I stood still while what just happened processed in my mind. When I looked back at the little gray house, I realized Craig had disappeared as fast as the ambulance.

It took me forever to climb our hill that day. I spent the night curled up on my window seat. I clutched the little porcelain moose for luck, and prayed my heart out for good news. Maybe there had been a mistake. Maybe Miss Cogshell was chuckling right now about the joke she had played.

My mom came in with a cup of cocoa. "You okay?" she asked. I nodded, unable to trust my voice. The cocoa went cold long after she left the room. I continued to stare out into the darkness. My weepy eyes turned the night sky into shooting stars.

❧ ❧ ❧

THREE DAYS LATER I sat with my mother at Miss Cogshell's funeral, held in her tiny church. After the series of small strokes, the most special old woman in my world had encountered a massive one—one she could not survive.

I was a wreck in my scratchy blue dress, waiting for the service to start. I whispered to my mother, "I don't know what to do."

"Why, you don't have to do anything." She patted my hand as the minister took his place at the front of the church. I peeked behind me one last time at the half-empty pews and spotted Craig's blond head coming in through the big arched doors. I didn't dare look at his face. I figured he'd sit at the back alone, but next thing I knew, I was shoving in to make room for him. I noticed the usual fresh grass scent of his jacket, mixed with a soapy smell.

Howard and Mary were there. Mary was one of several who stood up and spoke about Miss Cogshell. It made me wish I had known her even better.

"A lot of people in town had a problem with the books she used to assign to her students," said Mary, "but I'll tell you, that woman put the love of reading in us, well at least in me." She glanced at her husband with a warm smile.

"Howard used to sit behind me in her class and pull my braids. It was Miss Cogshell who gave me permission to turn around and sock him one if he ever did it again, but he never did." There was a trickle of chuckles and her husband's face turned crimson.

Craig and I exchanged looks. His hair was actually smoothed back like he had dragged a wet comb through it. The corner of his mouth twitched. I think we both remembered Howard's red face on the day we let Pup go.

"Anyone else?" asked the minister.

Craig's leg started bouncing beside me and a minute later he was standing at the front of the church in that old army jacket.

"I don't, I mean . . . I'm not used to churches, but I just want to thank Miss C. for all she's done."

Craig glanced at Howard and then with a who-cares shrug, he started in on the story of finding a helpless little orphan seal pup. He told it well, right down to the last farewell splash. The first time he mentioned my name, he nodded at me and everyone turned to stare. My mother raised her eyebrows at me and then took my hand as I slid further down in the pew.

"So that's the whole story," he said with a laugh, glancing again at Howard, who shook his head in dismay. Then Craig looked around at the flowers, and the solemnness of the occasion seemed to hit him.

"She also helped me with personal things, and I'm gonna miss . . . " Craig's face crumpled.

A few coughs and sniffles sounded from the small congregation. I squeezed my eyes shut. The church became so silent I thought I could hear the beating of my heart, but it was Craig's sneakers pounding up the aisle, out the door.

For me, a gray cloud settled in the church despite the sunlight still pouring through the stained-glass windows. The organist accompanied a small choir, who sang:

Amazing Grace, how sweet the sound
That saved a wretch like me.
I once was lost, but now am found;
Was blind, but now I see.

I felt a big lump form in my throat and I wanted to cry, but I didn't let myself because I knew if I did, I might never stop. If I cried, I might be admitting Miss Cogshell was really gone and that I'd never see her again.

The hymns ended with a long *Amen* that seemed to go on forever, before the organ went silent. After the service, people said how nice it had been, how the flowers were beautiful, how lovely the casket was, and other stupid things.

I raced home, changed into my jeans, and then wandered down to the dock to clear my head.

Moist salt air rose from sun-splashed waves. I sat at the end of the pier, as usual, and kicked my feet. The ocean spread out before me and I thought about how it was always here waiting and always would be. Seagulls were still flying, fish still swimming. Just like when I was small. Just like they would be if I sat here again in fifty years. And in a hundred years, all new people, but still that old ocean would be slapping the shore.

As I was about to leave I noticed a small black ball bobbing far off to my left. Then another further out. Old tires perhaps. The first one moved closer. Were my eyes playing tricks on me? I stood up and raised my hand to block the sun. My breath came faster. I walked backwards, not taking my eyes off the object. I leapt off the pier and ran to the little beach just as he was reaching the shore.

"Pup! Is it really you?" I knelt down and spread my arms wide. He hesitated. The little heart shape above his left eye sparkled in the sun. He nuzzled me and nipped my arm. I pulled his heavy body close and held him for a brief moment before he wiggled and splashed with two strong flippers. The cool water struck me and dripped into my eyes. I dashed it away.

When I could see clearly again, Pup was further out in the water beside the other shape. Yes, there were two! Another seal, a bit smaller and darker than Pup was by his side.

"Oh, Pup, I'm so happy for you." Tears of relief finally pushed the sad tears out. I cried. And cried.

Pup and his friend splashed around a while and then took off. "Come back again, Pup," I called. "I love you!"

19

I WENT AROUND in a daze for the first two weeks of summer vacation.

One night, bored out of my brain, I glanced at the local newspaper. It was filled with articles about the annual port picnic. Our town picnic was always held in the field down on the other side of the pier, across from Miss Cogshell's house. I supposed I would go. All of Port Wells turned out each 4th of July. There was usually watermelon and three-legged races. That sort of thing. For the last few years they had added a small stage and hooked up a microphone to a generator, so people could sing and dance and make fools of themselves. It was usually pretty funny.

There was also an interesting story in the news about a project where young puffins were being transplanted from Newfoundland to Eastern Egg Rock, a tiny island in Maine. I smiled. New little friends for Pup.

I skimmed an article about Skylab 1. The three astronauts were back from a record breaking 28 days in space. A month ago when they were sent up, I had thought it wasn't really such a long time. Now I realized a lot could happen in a month.

I turned to the next page of the newspaper and spotted a public auction notice. The small blurry photo below the notice showed none of the beauty of the little house by the sea. I thought I was going to be sick. How could the town sell Miss Cogshell's special home to just anybody? I threw down the paper and ran to find my father.

Dad was in his study, as usual, and we had strict orders not to disturb him when the door was closed. Except for emergencies. I turned the knob after a quick knock.

He placed his index finger on the work in front of him, slid his glasses further down his nose and then greeted me over the top of them with a *this had better be important* look. "Yes?"

I foolishly begged him to buy the house, sharing one wild scheme after another. "We could even rent it out to vacationers," I insisted.

He shook his head. "I'm sorry, Amy. There's just no way I could afford another place even if I wanted to. And that house has definitely seen better days." His finger hovered over his papers and I knew he wanted to get back to work.

It was no use. I closed the office door quietly behind me. Then I went to my room and climbed onto my window seat.

The next day, early, before anyone else was up, I ran down the hill. The salty air was dense with morning fog. A startled heron flapped its way out of the marshy area by the beach. Tears streamed down my face as I watched it soar overhead. It had been a long night.

I plunked myself down on Miss Cogshell's back steps. Only a few withered blossoms clung to the lilac bush, but the lupines were going strong. Their bright rainbow spikes let out a peppery scent.

My head ached as I dwelled on my problems. The auction was set for July 10th. What could I do to stop it? I closed my eyes and pictured the inside of the house. I went through each room with its special things. I thought of all those books, just lying there rotting. A plan formed in the back of my mind.

LUCKILY, CRAIG ANSWERED on the first ring or I probably would have chickened out and hung up. It had been a while since we'd talked. He was thrilled to hear I had seen Pup and his pal at the pier. Then, I blurted my scheme of how to save Miss Cogshell's house. I finally stopped to take a breath and heard silence. Even over the phone lines he could make my face redden. "I guess it's a stupid idea," I said.

"No," said Craig quickly. "I'm just thinking you should announce it at the picnic next week."

"Announce it? In front of the whole town? Yeah, right."

"I'm serious," said Craig, "If you tell them just the way you told me, it might work. And there's not much time. I was down at Al's this morning and some city people came in talking about Miss C's house. They wanna tear it down and squish in a hotel."

"That's stupid," I snapped. "A hotel wouldn't fit on that little . . . "

I heard Craig's mother yell in the distance.

"I've gotta go," said Craig, and he hung up. I wondered about his mom and decided I would ask about her when I saw him at the picnic. In the meantime I had to figure this out.

I went up to my room and started pacing, just like in the cartoons. Part of me said, "They are not going to get her house." My other half said, "Forget it, there's no way a stringy-haired kid is going to make any difference." One thing I knew for sure was I couldn't make a town announcement. I finally decided to find Craig at the beginning of the picnic and convince him to give the speech.

Day after day I moped around my room. I didn't read any books, or do any cross-stitching. I sat in my window seat, stared out into the backyard, and waited for the picnic—my only hope.

My exasperated parents threatened to send me off to summer camp.

"This one has lots of activities for girls *and* boys," said my mother. "Oh, when I was your age I dreamed of going to a co-ed camp." Mom got a faraway look on her face while she went off in a reverie of canoe races, crafts, and campfires.

But I couldn't snap out of it. All I could think about was Miss Cogshell's beautiful home getting smashed to smithereens.

Even Nancy attempted to be nice to her poor, sorrowful sister. I caught her looking at me the day before the picnic. She shook her head, her pink lips in a frown.

"Remember we used to play beauty parlor?" she said.

I nodded.

"How about I'll wash and trim your hair. And while it's drying, I'll paint your nails!"

I eyed her suspiciously. "You just want to fix me up."

"Well, yeah-h."

Since I had nothing better to do, I went along with it. Well, except for the nail polish part. Nancy set me up at the kitchen sink. I relaxed under her competent hands and enjoyed the smell of the green-apple shampoo. Then we moved to the middle of the kitchen with a towel around my shoulders. With each snip of the scissors I worried I would end up looking like the Dutch boy on the paint cans. But, in the end, I didn't look half bad.

"Well, it's the best I can do," said Nancy.

"With what you had to work with." I finished the saying under my breath and rolled my eyes.

I was pleased and grateful for my new look, though. Nancy used so much shampoo that I could almost call my hair fluffy, and being cut blunt gave it a little thickness. Every time I passed by a mirror, I gave my head an extra swing. Now to just get through tomorrow.

20

ON JULY 4TH, I put on a red striped T- shirt to go with my blue shorts, and headed down to breakfast.

"How sweet," said Nancy. She wore super short, purple paisley, hot-pants with a matching halter and looked about ten years older than me.

"Backatcha," I snapped, pretending to gag. Mom was busy gathering up craft items for the bazaar table.

I rushed through my bowl of cereal. Then, I headed down the hill towards the field to see what was going on. A strong sea smell filled the air. Long red, white, and blue banners were draped along the edge of the post office roof. Large tables were set up and little kids decorated their bikes with streamers. Chairs had been placed along the road to reserve prime spots for parade viewing. Although with half of the Port in the parade and the other half watching, there was hardly a need to save seats. If you couldn't see in one place, just move up a bit. Oh, well, must be the summer people leaving the chairs. They usually tended to keep their city ways, to show they were used to much fancier affairs.

Around 11:00 the parade lined up and began to march. A sad little band was in the lead with about a dozen out-of-tune members. Then came our one and only clown leaping around to make up for the lack of more performers. Each time the boom of the bass drum sounded, he jumped in surprise. Next came kids doing cartwheels or pulling pets in wagons. Then a bunch more on their decorated bikes. A few moms ran along the side. They yelled at the kids to go slow, so they wouldn't run anyone over or bump into the band. As usual, they didn't think to let the bikes go first.

At the tail end of the parade was Port Wells' pride and joy—an antique LaFrance fire engine. Chief Sorensen waved from one of the side footholds. Most of us covered our ears until the blaring siren moved past. Then a welcome pause of silence.

When I heard more music coming up at the rear I got excited for a minute, then I remembered it was just the first band over again. Duh, I'm fooled every year. They always went up the road past the general store and post office, turned right and then came back around in a circle. Sometimes they circled around three or four times. Everybody cheered and waved just as hard as the first two rounds. I bounced up and down on my tiptoes in search of Craig. No sight of him.

The sun was beating down hot by noon, so I wandered over to the shady edge of the field to see if the wild blueberries were ripe yet. Nope, still small and white. I plunked down on the blanket my parents had spread out on the grass before they went off to mingle.

My gaze fell fondly on Miss Cogshell's home across the way. I wished Craig would hurry up and show his face, so we could plan his speech. If only we could save the little house from destruction. I sat there swatting mosquitoes and smelling that good charcoal smell, until someone rang the dinner bell.

We all got in line at the food tables. The grub was always delicious at Port Wells picnics. I had three chickens on a stick and heaps of potato salad.

Later, I slurped down watermelon while I watched people play games and run races. Several fishermen were actually taking the day off, catching up on local news, chewing tobacco and spitting the brown juice into the grass. An ice cream truck played a tinny jingle of Pop Goes the Weasel as it pulled right onto the field to await customers.

I might have considered it one of the best 4th of July celebrations yet, if I weren't so worried about the house auction. Because of the big turnout this year, I still couldn't find Craig. Each time I thought I saw the top of his head, he'd disappear again.

Finally, Ed Johnson started tapping the microphone. "Testing one, two, three," he said. "All performers please wait to the right of the stage." I looked over and saw Pamela Johnson was first in line. I could feel my sweaty hair plastered to the back of my neck, but she looked cool and crisp in a perky little bun. Every year, Pamela opened up the show with "The Star Spangled Banner." That would have been fine if she could sing. Don't get me wrong, I wasn't just being jealous; she really and truly stunk.

I continued to search for Craig. I began to panic. Where *was* he? He'd said he liked my idea, and it would be nothing for him to talk in front of an audience—unlike me, who would probably pass out if I had to speak. People began to fill in around the stage and it became harder to see anything. The performer line grew longer as I raced back and forth searching.

I decided to go over and save a place in line for Craig, so he'd have a slot to announce our proposal. I squeezed through the crowd while everyone watched two little girls do cartwheels. I stood in back of a kid with juggling sticks. After each person finished, Mr. Johnson gave the next performer a nudge and made us all move up.

"I'm just waiting for someone," I told him.

"Okay, move forward," he said, as if he hadn't heard me. My stomach started feeling funny, and I wished I hadn't eaten so much.

Before I knew it, the kid with the juggling sticks was on stage and I was up on the steps, next in line. I started to sweat, hunting everywhere for Craig among the crowd of faces. Then I heard clapping and felt Mr. Johnson nudge me onto the platform. I tried to turn around and go back down the same stairs, but they were filled with newly arrived kids waiting to perform. My heart pounded as I took the few paces over to the microphone.

I was about to say I was up there by mistake, but no words came out. I made a tight fist with both hands, a trick I had read about in a book, and then I opened them slowly. This was supposed to help you calm down, although I couldn't tell if it worked. I looked out past the faces, and my eyes fell on Miss Cogshell's little house and that is when I began to relax. It seemed like Miss Cogshell, a smiling plump angel, was watching me from somewhere. I wanted to show her what I could do.

"We have lost one of our kindest citizens," I began, trying to copy the way the minister had spoken.

"Speak up!" someone shouted. I tucked my newly trimmed hair behind my ears and moved closer to the microphone.

"Miss Cogshell knew lots about everything. She was born in Port Wells, grew up in Port Wells and died in Port Wells." I looked out at the faces and landed on the harbormaster and his church-going wife. "She taught and worshiped with many in this community." I bit my lip and took another breath. I whispered, "Miss

Cogshell loved Port Wells." The microphone carried my words out over the silent crowd. "And she loved her home," I added, pointing at the little gray house. "There is a rumor that strangers want to tear down her home and build a big, ugly hotel."

I could hear murmuring as I poured out my heart. "But . . . but we can save it. The reason Miss Cogshell knew lots about everything is because there are hundreds of books in her home. Ones that she would want shared and we . . . " I paused. "We need a library. Why should we drive all the way to Thomaston when we can have our own library right here?"

My gaze landed on Pamela and memories of my oral book report disaster swam over me. But this time, Pamela wasn't smirking. I continued in a stronger voice. "I'm sure many of us have extra books we could donate and I'll work in the library every day, if you can just help me save this local treasure." The audience remained silent as if waiting for more.

I didn't know what to do. My eyes began to water. I heard clapping and followed the sound past the people sprawled out on blankets, past the lawn chairs, to the back of the crowd. A blurry Craig was standing on an upturned trashcan. His bike was propped against the side of the barrel below him. Others began to clap too, until there was a burst of applause.

A sturdy girl, about my age, stood at the front of the crowd. I'd never seen her before. She waved a small

American flag high above her head and cheered, "Yay for a new library! Yay for a new library!"

I stood dumbfounded for a moment and then groped my way down the stage steps. I didn't look to the right where my family stood, Nancy gawking for sure, or towards the left at Pamela's crew. I just plowed straight ahead to the back. My mind kept going over the last five minutes. I should have said thank you at the end, but I'd forgotten. By the time I reached Craig, I thought I'd burst out crying—my emotions were that full. He wore a big, sloppy grin and he was waving a long piece of paper around.

"Signatures," he called out, "almost a hundred so far."

I arranged my shaking face in a questioning look, unable to speak.

"All people in favor of a library. I've been working the crowd for an hour." Craig gave me the paper. His warm fingers brushed against my bare arm, and then he stuck his hands into the pockets of his army jacket. I couldn't believe he was still wearing it.

I wasn't sure I could trust my voice yet, but finally blurted out, "Aren't you sweltering? I mean it must be 85 degrees."

"I'm fine." Craig gave another grin, but it didn't reach his eyes.

"How's your mom?" I remembered to ask.

"Fine," Craig answered. "I've gotta get back . . . " Loud clapping for an accordion player interrupted us, and then a tap dance group took their place on stage. I watched them and tried to come up with something else to say to Craig—something to make up for the last two questions.

People started moving away from the stage area as the last performance ended. A group of big kids strolled past us. I could see purple paisley in the middle of them. "That was my sister," I heard Nancy say. I turned back to Craig, but he was gone.

For the rest of the day, people came up to me and told me what a great idea I had, and how they would help however they could. I had them sign the petition if they hadn't already. But I wasn't sure what I should do with it. Who could I give it to?

One woman said she had been trying to get a library in the Port for years. "Sylvia's house might offer the perfect solution," she said, eyeing my list of signatures. "My name is Mrs. Baldwin. What are you planning to do with that petition?"

I looked down at all the names and let out a small sad sigh. "I'm not really sure."

"I'd be happy to help you present it to town officials, if you'd like. Then, if they approve your idea for a library, we can enlist a group of people to help."

"Thank you," I said with gratitude and relief. We made plans to meet first thing Monday morning.

As the picnic neared the end, I wandered down to the pier where it would be slightly cooler, navigating past three spinning little girls with sparklers in their outstretched hands. I searched the water and wondered how Pup was doing. I would have liked to talk to Craig about him.

21

I COULDN'T BELIEVE it when the following week an announcement in the newspaper said the public auction had been cancelled and that Miss Cogshell's house would become the Port Library. So I guess you could say I got the ball rolling, and with the help of Mrs. Baldwin and all the people who signed the petition, it was really going to happen.

A few of the town big shots organized a select group to clean out her house.

One day, while I was hanging around at home, trying hard not to think about what they might be doing with Miss Cogshell's special things, there was a knock on the door.

An unfamiliar woman stood on the front stoop. She held a shoebox. "You're Amy Henderson, correct?" I nodded. "We found a card with your name on it stuck inside Sylvia's cabinet. So, here you go. I wrapped them as best I could."

I thanked her and relieved her of the box.

"Oh." She looked down at another small card. "Do you know Craig Miller?"

"Yes," I said.

"Where does he live?"

I gave her directions and then asked, my breath rate picking up speed, "Is there something I could deliver?"

"No thank you, dear. It's just an old cuckoo clock and I've got the car here." With that she was on her way.

Soon I was pulling out one miniature china animal after another from the crinkly balls of tissue paper. I would cherish them forever. As I carefully unwrapped the fragile figurines, I remembered how Miss Cogshell had come by most of them—the little penguin from her adventurous college friend, a miniature trio of piglets from the farmer's wife, and a big-eyed turtle from a favorite student years ago. All of the tiny figures stood at only an inch or less. The smallest was a mouse with glossy pink ears. I was anxious to reintroduce my repaired moose to the group. Maybe I would find a little seal someday, one that I could add to the collection in memory of Pup.

THERE WAS THIS gigantic committee formed to remodel the house into a library. As promised, I spent every day attaching routing slips to books and then stamping the ones people wanted to borrow. There were so many donated volumes that we had to put shelves in the bedrooms too. Crammed with several new bookcases, the kitchen became the check-out-station. There were big plans to refurnish everything; however, it would take time and money. Clyde, Miss Cogshell's walking stick, had a permanent lookout position on the wall near the aquatic reptile books.

After the initial busyness, things quieted down, and I had more time to sit at the check-out desk, staring out the back door past the shriveled lilac bush. I would often plug in a little fan and direct it right on me. Although usually cooler in Maine, the temperature was unbearable that summer. Pine needles turned pale as they baked in the heat.

On days when the town beach looked more inviting, there were hardly any patrons, but a few regulars began hanging out in their chosen corners. The husky girl who had cheered for a new library after my 4th of July speech, came in a lot. She wore granny glasses and the thick braid that fell past her waist swung as she walked. I'd often see her over in the back corner snuggled up in Miss Cogshell's old blue chair, feet tucked up beneath her as she read.

I kept thinking Craig might stop by. I had found it hard to come to Miss Cogshell's house the first few times and I wondered if maybe it was even harder for him. It had become a comfortable place for me to hang out now, though; and I was sure she'd be thrilled to see what her home had turned into.

While I worked in the silent library day after day, I realized it really was okay to be alone. Who needed crowds around to feel popular? I mean, I'd always have me and my own dreams. After spending time in Miss Cogshell's special house, I was beginning to know what those dreams were. No matter how life changed around me, no one could take them away. Maybe I'd surprise myself and I *would* go to college someday. Maybe I'd become a librarian, or a mystery writer, or even a great explorer. Yeah that's it, my zits would go away and so would I.

On my way home each day, I would often stop at the pier, searching the vast water for signs of Pup and hoping Craig would think to do the same. Almost hoping the three of us could do it all again. But only I showed up. I made sure I got through the woods before sundown each night, placing my footsteps with care to avoid moose poop on lime-green sneakers.

ONE OF THOSE hot August mornings, after an hour of no customers, my sister came into the library to look around for the first time.

"Whooee, how can you stand it in here?" Nancy fluttered her polished nails toward her face.

I shrugged while she continued to browse. I had this feeling she was up to more than looking at books since they were never really her thing. Either way, it was fun to show off how much we had done to make it look like a real library.

"Ya know, I wanted to ask you something, Amy," she said.

Okay, here it comes.

"I happened to see that friend of yours a few minutes ago, Miller is it?"

I glanced fast at the door, hoping to see Craig after all these weeks.

Nancy doesn't miss much. "Oh, he's probably gone by now," she said. "Anyway, I've just got to ask you. You and him are just friends, right? I mean you're not really going out or anything, are you?"

A while ago I would have gotten all embarrassed, but I wasn't about to let that happen this time, so I said, "Yeah, just friends."

"That's what I figured." Nancy gave a knowing smile, as she flipped through an upside down copy of *The Grapes of Wrath*. "When I asked him about you at the town picnic, he acted kind of odd."

"You what?" I shrieked.

Nancy smiled again, ever patient. "Well, he was going up to everyone getting them to sign his paper, so I figured it was a perfect opportunity to ask him what was happening between you two."

My face must have turned a thousand colors, but my anger was stronger. "You had no right . . . " I stopped, forcing myself not to give her what she wanted. Besides, I had an overwhelming desire to know what Craig had said. No way would I ask though.

Nancy waited while I pretended to straighten some cards. "Funny thing is," she finally said, creasing her smooth brow, "he wouldn't answer me. He just had this huge smile on his face." She sauntered towards the door. "Oh, well, it's too hot in here for me. But it's a cute little library," she tossed back over her shoulder, and then she added, "almost as cute as that Miller kid."

I grinned and adjusted my fan.

TWENTY MINUTES LATER the door swung open again. And there he was.

"Hi Craig," I managed.

"Amy," he said, one foot still stuck in the threshold. His Adam's apple moved up and down while he took in every corner of Miss Cogshell's converted kitchen. "I wasn't sure how it would look," he finally said.

"And . . . " I said.

"Looks pretty good." His voice seemed a little lower than when I had seen him last. Then the familiar grin surfaced when he added, "Almost like a library."

"That's the whole idea," I said, grinning back. I wondered why he was staring at me that way.

Craig shoved his damp bangs, still long, but bleached lighter, up off his flushed face. "I woulda come by sooner if I'd had the time."

"Looks like you've had lots of sun," I said.

"Yeah. Been cutting lawns all summer. Gives me plenty of thinking time, ha, too much thinking time. I go back to when me and you would just hang out, sometimes with Miss C. or with Pup, but mostly I think about some of them deep talks we had." Craig laughed. "I wasn't used to that—ya know, the way you listen and analyze everything, like you actually care what I might think about stuff."

Craig turned away, peered down the hall and then blurted out, "Actually I came to see you, to tell you something."

I swallowed and started fidgeting with a paperclip.

"Remember I said my mom was going into a treatment center?"

I nodded.

"Well she kept changing her plans, but with a little push from the social worker, tomorrow's the day." Craig tried to match my smile, his piercing eyes a smoky gray in the dim light. "It's far away," he continued, "and they won't let kids stay home alone."

"Where will you go?" I held my breath.

"I have an aunt in Boston. She'll take me in, and my little brother and sisters will go to another aunt in Portland."

"Boston," I whispered, biting my lip, as the paperclip slipped to the floor. My face must have gone pale, because Craig moved closer to me.

"It won't be for long. I'll be back." He still watched me with the most serious expression I'd ever seen on him. "Get up, Amy."

"What?" I asked, rising.

"Come over here." He glanced out the window and quietly closed the inside storm door.

I moved over to him as if in a trance. My head almost reached his shoulder as he pulled me close into a hug.

"Don't know why, but I've always wanted to do this," he said softly in my ear, his voice low and different.

I'm sure he could feel my body trembling through my tie-dye T-shirt, but all I felt was that big old army jacket. I knew I was going to start crying and I didn't care. This was my last chance with Craig. I wrapped my arms around him.

We stayed that way for a while until the sounds of someone coming down the walkway reached us. Just as we broke apart, Craig whispered, "I'll send you my address."

I looked at him doubtfully.

"I promise. I will write," he said. "Hey, maybe I'll even write you a song." He grinned the grin I'd never forget. "That may take a while, but I'll figure it out."

Sally Johnson came bustling in, glancing from one to the other of us. "That door should be open," she said. "You need some air in here, and I need a book about birds. And I've only got a minute; Pammy's watching the post office for me."

I started to reach for Miss Cogshell's old bird book on the third shelf up, when I heard Craig leave. I spun around to find the screen door still swinging and him already gone. Sally continued to chatter.

"It's about time we had our own library, Amy. It is Amy, isn't it? I thought so. You didn't do half bad getting this going." Then she stopped talking and peered at me, "Are you okay?"

I nodded and checked out the book for her, glad when the door finally swung shut behind her. Then I rushed to the back of the house and all the way up the narrow steps to the widow's walk to check if Craig was down at the pier. No sign of him. I searched in the other direction, only to see the retreating back of Sally Johnson returning to the post office. Dragging my feet, I went back down through the stifling heat. That's when I noticed there was something on my chair.

I picked up the photo of two kids hugging a seal. Craig must have developed Miss Cogshell's pictures and left this here for me.

The library door opened once more. The girl with the long braid came in. She smiled at me and headed for the mystery section. I looked down again at the photo. Studying it, I knew I would always be able to feel the texture of Pup's fur beneath my hands, smell the seaweed, hear the ocean waves, and see the brilliance of Craig's smile, a boy hiding in a big army jacket, whom I almost got to know really well. Who'd a thought it?

I took a deep breath, walked over to the new girl and in my strong new voice, said "Hi, I'm Amy."

About the Author

Marcia Strykowski has always felt a connection to the ocean and its creatures. She has adopted a puffin named Abigale through Project Puffin, and more recently adopted a harbor seal from World Wildlife Fund. When she's not watching the waves, she works at a public library. After numerous magazine and anthology contributions, *Call Me Amy* is her first novel.